Mason

Morris Fenris

Mason, Three Brothers Lodge #2

Copyright 2015 Morris Fenris

Changing Culture Publications

Table of Contents

Chapter 1

Sunday before Thanksgiving, just above Silver Springs, Colorado…

"Gracie, did anyone happen to check the weather report before we headed up here?" Becca Edwards asked, watching the ever darkening sky with a sense of trepidation. She liked nature, but her experience of being in the mountains during a storm of any kind was more than limited. It was non-existent.

The gathering black and grey clouds were alarming, and they seemed to be getting closer and lower with each passing moment. A storm was brewing, and they were fixing to get caught right in the middle of it.

"Sure I did. They were expecting maybe a few snow flurries tonight and tomorrow, but nothing big," Melanie Jenkins, now Melanie Walters, told her. "It's not supposed to get real bad until next week."

Melanie and Becca had become best friends when they'd become roommates at college four years earlier. Melanie had been a business major while Becca was a journalism major, specializing in outdoor photography. She was currently hoping to land a job as a wildlife photographer with the Division of Wildlife.

To that end, she needed some spectacular outdoor shots of the Colorado Mountains. She and Melanie had hiked in these mountains many times over the last few years, and being that Melanie was headed across the country to work in her father's company the day after Thanksgiving, they had decided to make this last minute trip.

Melanie had gotten married three months earlier to her high school sweetheart via the Internet. Her husband, Master Chief Michael Walters, had just returned from his second tour in Afghanistan, and was currently undergoing a debriefing period in

Colorado Springs. He was due to get his discharge papers at the end of the month. At that point in time, Melanie and her husband would be moving to Florida, and Becca was afraid that she'd never see her best friend again.

The third member of the hiking group was Gracie Shelton. She was a seasoned hiker and climber, and up until a month ago, their third roommate. The three had been together for several years, and shared a bond and sisterhood only friends who had weathered life's storms together could appreciate.

Gracie, unlike the others who had grown up in a city environment, had grown up in Silver Springs, although she'd been gone since she was fourteen. Her parents had moved to the Denver area just before she entered high school, and while she'd never been back to visit, a part of her heart had always remained in Silver Springs, given to a teenage boy her age when they were much too young to understand that life didn't always work out the way they wanted it to.

Now she was back, and ready to check out the small town. Gracie was in a class by herself, having skipped ahead in her schooling after leaving Silver Springs; she'd graduated from high school with two years of college already accomplished at seventeen. She'd gotten accepted into medical school at nineteen, and at the age of twenty-two, was now ready to begin her career.

She'd graduated from medical school a few months back, and been prepared to work as an emergency room physician while she decided if she wanted to specialize or just practice family medicine. She'd been having a hard time deciding just where she wanted to practice or what kind of medicine she wanted to do; nothing appeared to fit or feel right.

Then she'd seen the ad for a doctor in Silver Springs. It seemed that Doc Matthews was getting ready to retire, but hadn't told anyone in town yet. He wanted to bring in a fresh young doctor, to work alongside him over the next six months. Then he would step out of the picture, allowing the new doctor a chance at owning their own practice in the small mountain town.

It was a dream come true, and she'd immediately emailed him her resume. She had explained about having grown up in Silver Springs, and Doc had immediately inquired about both of her parents, having recognized her surname. He'd delivered her, along with half of the town, and it seemed that he never forgot a name.

She'd had several phone conversations with the man over the last two months, and it had been decided that she would start on December first. She hadn't gotten very far into her planning for the move when she had overheard Becca and Melanie talking about making a trip to Maroon Peak. Since it was directly above Silver Springs, she'd asked if she could tag along, and had laughed at the look of relief on both women's faces. They both liked the outdoors well enough, but when it came to serious hiking, they were amateurs and they knew it. Gracie did not fit into that category.

She had contacted Sarah and made arrangements for her and her two friends to stay there for a few nights. Melanie was driving to Colorado Springs on Wednesday to spend the holiday weekend with her husband, and though Gracie had asked Becca numerous times about her plans, her hurting friend had been very quiet and noncommittal. Gracie was hoping she could get Becca to open up to her during this trip.

A gust of wind drew her attention skyward, and she watched the storm clouds gather over the mountain. A sense of urgency to seek shelter assailed her, and she knew that the chances of them making it down the mountain before nightfall were slim. At least, not without some assistance. The sunlight was completely hidden by the dark clouds, and the air temperature was dropping fast. The sky had been blue when they first set out on their hike, but two hours later, it was hard to remember what it looked like. They were in trouble, and needed to get back to town. Immediately.

There were several problems with that though. It was the Sunday before Thanksgiving, and they'd passed no other hikers or campers in the area. On top of that, they were currently on the opposite side of the mountain from the closest cell tower, meaning that they had absolutely no cell phone service.

None of them had short-wave radios with them, and Gracie mentally kicked herself for not having the foresight to stick one in her camping pack. She knew better, having grown up on the mountain, but this trip had been a hurried last attempt to help Becca get some pictures, and she hadn't taken the proper precautions before leaving Denver. She only hoped they wouldn't all pay a hefty price for that mistake.

They couldn't even call for help from their present location. Deciding that it was time to speak up and try to salvage this trip, she got Becca's attention, "We need to head down."

"But I haven't gotten the shots I want yet." The park ranger had told them there was a nest of eagles at the top of the Northern Trailhead, and had described the location of their nest. That was their current goal, but not one they were going to see today.

Of the three women, Becca was the least likely of their group to handle a difficult hike down. Six months previously, she'd been attacked while walking across a parking garage late at night, and since then she'd been different. No longer confident or willing to take any sort of risk, the fact that she'd wanted to come up on this mountain had been what Gracie saw as an attempt to return to normal.

Becca had healed physically, but mentally and emotionally, she seemed to be suffering from what Gracie thought was classic PTSD. Night terrors. Jumpy in strange situations. Being stuck atop a mountain in the middle of a winter storm was not something she would handle well, or at all. She'd been prone to panic attacks since the attack, and Gracie didn't even want to think about having to talk her down from one of those while also fighting Mother Nature.

She did seem to listen to Gracie, turning to her for help and support, but Gracie knew what she had to offer wasn't enough. She had tried to get her to attend some group counseling sessions, but Becca had adamantly refused, saying she was handling everything just fine and didn't need to share her emotional meltdowns with a bunch of strangers. She was hoping to find the young woman someone to help her before she left town, but so far, that hadn't occurred. Becca was handling things on her own, and in her own way, and Gracie's biggest fear was that once she left Denver, Becca would completely shut down and isolate herself away from society. That would be detrimental to her ever recovering from the attacks and living a normal life.

She met Becca's gaze and told her, "I know that you wanted more time to shoot up here, but those clouds aren't going to go away. And if we don't get over to the other side of the mountain before nightfall, no one's even going to know we're up here. Trust me; we don't want that to happen." The park ranger would know they'd come up, and if she looked, she'd see her vehicle in the parking area, but those were pretty big ifs, and Gracie would rather save herself than depend upon a stranger to do so.

Melanie looked at the sky and nodded, "I think she's right, Becca. We really do need to retrace our steps. Maybe we can find someplace to shelter for the night, and come back and get your shots in the morning? We have enough food and water to last through the night."

Gracie shook her head at the foolish comment. It was evident that Melanie had only been in the mountains during the Summer and early Fall. This was neither, and a winter storm was on its way.

"That's not going to work. We aren't prepared to survive out here overnight. Not in this type of weather."

"We have the tent and can make a fire..."

Gracie shook her head, "Melanie, we'd never keep a fire going unless it was inside the tent, and you've done enough camping to know that isn't even a possibility. On top of that, our sleeping bags are in the vehicle, which is at the base of this mountain. It's going to snow, and get much colder than it is now. We need to head down before that happens, or at least be on our way down."

Gracie wasn't going to spend any more time arguing the point. She was right, and she was prepared to do whatever she could to make sure they made it off this mountain in one piece.

"Look, I'm going to hike back down to the trailhead below. You two go around the same way we came and I'll meet you there after I get a hold of the forest service dispatch in town." They'd passed a cut wall a hundred yards back. It would lead down to the lower trail, and then she would be only a half mile or so from where she could call for help. She could easily handle the climb down. Her friends would freak when they saw the rock wall and how far down the bottom was.

Becca looked alarmed, "Is it really that dangerous for us to be up here?"

"Not right now, but in another hour or so, things are going to get pretty nasty. There was an overhang just beyond that rock slide. Wait there for me, and then we'll hike down together." She tried to downplay the danger so that Becca wouldn't spin off into a panicked state, but she also didn't want them thinking they could lollygag around. They needed to get moving. Now!

"Why don't you just come with us?" Becca asked, a note a panic in her voice that Gracie immediately tried to quell.

Gracie smiled, "I grew up here, remember. I'm a much better hiker and can move faster on my own. I'll hike down, make the call, and then meet you. With any luck, they'll have a team in the area to come up and help us get back down the mountain tonight. They might even get to the overhang before you two do."

She looked once again at the gathering storm clouds, and only hoped she'd make it down to call for help before things got really bad. A few light snow flurries were already starting to fall from the sky. "You all need to head down. Now."

Gracie turned to leave and Melanie called her back, "What happens if you don't meet us?"

Gracie swallowed her sense of dread, and then smiled and told her solemnly, "Then you two continue following the trail down and make the call. Tell them I need help. You can play rescuer to my damsel in distress."

When she saw the look on Becca's face, she quickly added, "But I'm going to be fine. Don't worry about me. I've not worried. Just get to that overhang and I'll get help on the way."

She headed off, diving off the edge of the cliff fifty yards back and scrambling her way down until she reached the next level area. She was breaking all of the rules of outdoor survival by taking off on her own, but Becca and Melanie were both amateur hikers, and there was no way they could have handled her current hike down. That would have been asking for disaster.

She paused at the top of the wall and pulled on her gloves. They were fingerless and would help her grip the rock crevices and hold her weight as she looked for footholds and such, but would still protect her tender palms from being cut. The first ten feet were easy, nicely weathered, and she had no trouble finding a place to put her toes or her fingers. But hallway down, she found herself having to use all of her skills to negotiate her way down the last thirty feet of rock wall.

She was once again thankful for the rock climbing gym she'd joined just out of high school. She'd wanted to join earlier, but her father hadn't wanted her doing anything that was reminiscent of their time in Silver Springs. She frowned, wishing that she and her father had been able to settle their differences before his passing. It had been two years now, and she still harbored some bitterness towards the man who'd uprooted their family just because she'd gone and fallen in love with a young man he didn't think suitable. At least, that was the misconception she'd operated under, before realizing there was another issue at hand.

It had taken her several years before she'd finally gotten to the root of the problem. The ugly truth had finally come out after her father was diagnosed with a failing heart. Years earlier, he'd violated his marriage vows and slept with a young woman from Silver Springs who only occasionally came back to town. She'd been trying to get her life together, and doing a credible job, but then she'd gone and fallen for Gracie's father, Bill Shelton.

The woman had left town shortly after he'd realized what he was doing was wrong and hurting so many people. He'd never said anything to his wife, and then the woman had gone and gotten killed. He'd attended the funeral, along with the rest of the community, his sense of guilt over her death something that sat heavy on his shoulders.

He felt that the reason she'd left was due in part to their sinful dalliance. He'd been able to pretend that time in his life had never happened, watching silently from the wings as the woman's sons grew up, motherless, to become teenagers. He was viewed as an upstanding citizen in the community, and his pride had kept him from coming clean, and ridding himself of the guilt he carried around.

11

But when Gracie had fallen in love with one of the woman's sons, he'd been afraid of the truth coming out. He said he was trying to save his marriage, but Gracie knew he'd been trying to save himself from embarrassment. As a deacon on the church board, he'd been privy to confidential information about other church members, and many times Gracie had heard him belittle someone else's sin. Now he was the one caught, and he didn't want any of the punishment coming to him.

When he knew that his time on this Earth was short, he could no longer bear the guilt inside, and confessed all to Gracie and her mother. He'd been so afraid of his secret coming out as Gracie and Mason grew closer together, he'd run. Packing up the family, he took a position with a law firm in Denver, and moved everyone practically overnight.

Gracie had hated him for doing that. She'd had to leave all of her friends, and the only boy she'd ever truly cared about. *Mason Donnelly.* Her father hadn't even given her a chance to say goodbye. She'd simply come home from school to find a moving van in the driveway and a team of men loading the boxes they had just packed into the truck.

Her mother never complained, and after her father passed away, Gracie's mother confirmed that she'd known he been unfaithful to her, but she took her side of the wedding vows seriously and hadn't said anything because she didn't want to ruin the life they'd built together. She'd secretly forgiven him, long before he'd even confessed or asked for such. Gracie hadn't been able to understand that depth of forgiveness coming from another human. She knew that God was capable of forgiving that much, but she just couldn't see how a human could do so and not constantly be reminded of the past.

A strong gust of wind brought her attention back to the present. That sad time was over with, and she was here to make a new life for herself. She'd not dared ask Sarah about Mason or if he was still single, for fear of the answer. Mason was her other half. She'd known it when they were adolescents, and she still felt the same now.

When she'd made the decision to move to Silver Springs, she had reluctantly turned the situation over to God. She reasoned that if God hadn't allowed her feelings for Mason to dissipate over the course of eight years, that maybe God knew something she didn't. She'd prayed and asked Him to only bring Mason back into her life if they had a future together. She didn't want either of them to get hurt, and it was only recently that she'd begun to have doubts regarding her father's infidelity. Mason and his brothers didn't know, and she really didn't have any intention of telling them. Or at least, she was trying to get to that point in her thinking.

Now, here she was, scrambling down the slippery face of a rock wall, hoping to reach a point where there would be cell service to phone and call for help before the storm blowing in trapped them on the mountain. She felt a sense of panic like never before, and was just about to make her final descent, when a gust of wind rose up out of nowhere. She was about twelve feet off the ground, and her strength was dwindling fast.

She grappled for the next handhold, but water had frozen in the crevice of the rocks and her fingertips only met ice. Slippery ice. Her hand lost its purchase on the rocks and she felt her feet leave the rock wall as she fell. The ground came up to meet her fast, her head bouncing on the ground as she landed painfully with her right leg twisted at an odd angle beneath her.

Excruciating pain radiated from her body, and she moaned in agony. Her head hurt something fierce and when she tried to focus her eyes, everything seemed blurry and as if it were hidden behind a shroud.

She tried to move, but the pain was intense and she felt struggled to breathe through it. She needed to get to a place where she could phone for help, but as her vision grew dark and her hands began to register the cold, she slipped into unconsciousness. The face of a young teenage boy hovered for a moment, and she silently sent out a plea to God to send help and save her. She planned to make Silver Springs her home for the next forty years or so, but first, she had to get down off this mountain!

Chapter 2

Pastor Jeremy had just finished his sermon on being thankful, ending the morning service with a prayer over the meal the church was about to consume. It was a tradition for the church congregation to come together the Sunday before Thanksgiving and share a meal after the morning service. Everyone brought something, based upon what letter their last name began with, and it gave them all a chance to socialize with one another before the busy holiday season kicked into full swing.

Jeremy moved through the congregants, keeping an eye on Justin's tall head as he did so. He'd not gotten a chance to greet Jessica Andrews yet, and he wanted to make sure that her presence had been noted and how welcome she was in their church. He headed down the center aisle, shaking hands and nodding his head to others as he did so.

This was the first time she'd come into the church, and from the look on Justin Donnelly's face, it was the perfect way to kick off the holidays. *Could Jessica finally be ready to admit what was in her heart?* He hoped so for Justin and her sakes.

He finally reached them and reached for her hand, "Jessica! It was so good to have you in service this morning."

"Thank, Pastor. It felt good to be here." She was smiling and looked completely at ease.

Jeremy looked at Justin and smiled, "You two look good together."

"Thanks." Justin looked at Jessica and then back to the pastor. Lowering his voice so that his words wouldn't carry far, he said, "I imagine we'll be coming to see you sometime in the near future. Just as soon as we work out a few more details."

Jeremy raised a brow, "Does that mean…"

Justin shook his head, "Not yet, but that's where this is going. Just thought I'd give you fair warning."

"Consider me duly warned." Jeremy turned back to Jessica, who was having a spirited conversation with some of his younger members of the congregation. Students from her classroom. He watched for a moment, pleased to see the rapport she had already developed with the next generation.

He tapped her on the shoulder and when she turned, he smiled, "Jessica, again, it was a pleasure. Enjoy lunch you two."

Mason and Kaillar had been standing off to the side and heard their brother's veiled remarks. Pulling Justin to the side, Kaillar asked, "Are you seriously considering marrying Jessica?"

Justin nodded his head, "Yes. I know it's too soon to ask her right now, but that won't always be the case."

Mason slapped him on the shoulder, "Well, just so you know, I'm fully on board with that idea. Jessica is great and she makes you smile."

"Thanks, brother. Now, let's go grab some food. I saw Mrs. Hathaway earlier walking into the kitchen with three different pies."

Kaillar rubbed his stomach and laughed, "I hope one of them is pecan. She makes it like nobody else I know."

Mason started to agree, but then the face of an angel from his past filled his vision. *Gracie Shelton.* The girl who'd stolen his heart at the beginning of high school and then left town without a word. Her mother had made the best pecan pie, and more than once, Gracie had snuck an extra piece out of the house and they'd had it with their lunch

He didn't know why he was thinking about her now, as he hadn't done so for a while. She'd been gone for more than eight years, but he smiled at the memory, and then pushed the hurt it left behind away. His Uncle Jed had spent many nights talking to him after she'd left. He'd finally come to terms with the fact that at the tender age of fourteen, Gracie was at the whimsy of her parents. She'd had no choice but to leave town when they did, and deep inside Mason had always hoped she'd come back. When she was an adult. That hope was still there, but he'd managed to bury it deep beneath the chores and responsibilities of day-to-day life.

Inwardly sighing, he pushed those memories aside. Today was a day for celebrating, not reminiscing about a past you couldn't change. A time to be thankful for the things you did have, not the things you didn't.

They all headed over to the kitchen area and Mason was just about to sit down and start eating when Sarah joined them with a worried look up on her face. The forty something widow owned and operated the only motel and boarding house in Silver Springs. She was as level-headed as they come, and seeing her so worried had all three men standing up and taking notice.

Kai was the first to speak up, "Hey Sarah. What's up? You look awfully worried for such a nice afternoon."

"I am worried. I have three young women who are supposed to be staying tonight, but they haven't called or shown up yet."

"They're probably just taking their time. Where were they coming in from?"

"Denver."

"Well, I wouldn't get too worried yet. Why were they coming up here?"

"Something about taking some pictures from the top of Maroon Peak."

"What?!" Mason exclaimed. "It's pure stupidity to think that you can climb Maroon Peak this time of year. Especially with a storm about to arrive."

"I know. I have a feeling that something is terribly wrong."

Mason wasn't one for believing in women's intuition, but in this instance, he felt a sense of urgency to locate the women and ensure that they were someplace safe and warm. Stepping to the side, he placed a quick phone call, and the sense of dread he felt magnified a hundredfold.

"Hey Kai! I just got off the phone with the ranger at the station. She said three women headed up to the top of Maroon Peak around ten o'clock this morning."

"What?! Why would they do that? Didn't they check the weather?" Kaillar, otherwise known as Kai to his family and friends, shook his head in disbelief. He and his brothers operated the only guide service and tourist lodge in the area. Maroon Peak was their stomping grounds.

The mountain was not an easy climb in good weather, and with a major winter storm due to roll in, no one should be up on the side of that mountain. Not intentionally, or even deliberately. The mountains could get nasty in a hurry, and even seasoned climbers knew better than to hike in this weather.

Kaillar, the middle of the three brothers, headed for the door to the outside, stepping back in a few seconds later, shaking the snowflakes from his hair. "It's getting pretty nasty out there already. Visibility on the mountain has got to be nil."

Mason raised a brow and then shook his head, muttering about stupid tourists and foolish women. Mason was twenty-two, with dark hair and deep blue eyes. He was also in charge of the local search and rescue team, and if there were two women lost on the mountain, it would fall to him and his brothers to find them.

"I hope they took shelter," he murmured, looking out the large picture window that overlooked the mountain beyond.

"What do you think?" Kaillar asked, taking a seat at a nearby table.

"Did the ranger happen to say which way they were going to ascend?"

"The Northern Trailhead. One of the women is a photographer and the park ranger told them about the eagle's nest at the top."

Mason nodded, "Wonderful." His voice laced with sarcasm that belied his words. "Well, at least that way has some flat ground about midway up. Hopefully they saw the storm clouds gathering and took shelter."

Justin nodded his head as well, "Think we should try to go find them before we lose the daylight?"

Mason and Kaillar looked at each other and then sighed. "Yeah. We'll go. You stay here and man the radio, just in case we find the worst."

Mason grabbed a plate and headed for the food tables, "Let me grab a piece of pie and we can head up to the cabin. We'll need our gear."

Kaillar joined him and a few minutes later, they were ready to head out. Sarah followed them out, and then pulled Mason aside.

"Mason, I think you should know that one of the women is Gracie Shelton."

Mason's eyebrows disappeared beneath his too-long hair, "What?"

Sarah nodded solemnly, "I just didn't want you to be surprised when you saw her." It was common knowledge that a much younger Mason had been enthralled with Gracie Shelton. It also hadn't escaped anyone's notice that he seemed to have changed once she left town. No longer the carefree teenager, getting into trouble and raising a ruckus. He'd become quieter, and more withdrawn. He'd also isolated himself from the rest of the female population. At least the single ones.

Even years later, his only female friends were either widows, cousins, or married. A fact the single women in the surrounding towns and Silver Springs lamented for far too often.

Sarah was sure it was because Gracie had taken his heart with her when she'd left, and she'd secretly prayed for the day when Gracie would be out from under her father's thumb and come back to Silver Springs where she belonged.

"What is Gracie doing back here?" Mason asked, keeping his voice level and without the emotion racing through him.

"Doc put an ad out to find a replacement physician. He says he's ready to retire. I understand Gracie just finished medical school a few months ago."

Mason said nothing, his mind still reeling from the fact that Gracie was back in Silver Springs. On Maroon Peak. In the way of a dangerous winter storm!

"Thanks for the warning. Kai, let's roll." Mason's desire to reach the women before the storm became too overwhelming had just raised ten notches.

The two men made short work of getting back to the cabin. Kaillar grabbed them some protein bars and water while Mason packed up the first aid kit, extra batteries for their flashlights, and some climbing gear. A short wave radio, rope, several thermal blankets, matches to start a fire with, and several C-rations completed their kits. They had no intention of being out on the mountain all night, but the first rule of survival in the mountains was to always be prepared for the worst, hope for the best, and deal with the hand you got to the best of your ability.

By 2:30 p.m., they were back in the truck and headed for the Northern Trailhead. The ranger was still waiting for them, and she described the vehicle and the three women in great detail. They'd passed the vehicle in the parking area, confirming the three women had not hiked down yet. They got detailed descriptions of each woman from the park ranger, and Mason knew. There was no doubt in Mason's mind that the blond woman described to him was Gracie. No doubt at all.

As a teenager, he'd begged God to bring Gracie back to him. Now that it appeared to have occurred, he found himself alternating between fear and jubilation. Kaillar was driving, having found the ATV trail that would take them partway up the mountain and save some much needed time. While he drove, Mason kept his gaze on the approaching mountain peak. If Gracie were up on the mountain, he would find her, hopefully before any harm could come to her. That was his mission; he only hoped that he'd be successful in making it a reality.

Chapter 3

Gracie felt icy water on her face and slowly opened her eyes, taking in the ominous clouds right overhead. Snow was already beginning to fall from them, in great big flakes that were full of moisture. Looking at the surrounding ground covered in the white stuff already, she knew it had been snowing for quite a while, a period of time where she'd lain unconscious on the hard ground.

She started to move, but pain radiated through her body, and she recalled falling from the rock face. She lay still and tried to take stock of the injuries to her body. Her ribs were achy, but not so much so that she worried about cracks or breaks. Just bruises were bad enough. Her head hurt, and when she lifted a hand to her temple, it came away with blood on it.

Moving down her body, she was freezing, her teeth chattering, and her arms feeling sluggish and heavy. Her mind felt slow, and she wondered how long she'd been lying there. It was starting to grow dark, but she couldn't tell if it was from the gathering storm clouds, or if the sun had already gone down behind the mountains.

Her back felt fine, and she gingerly tried to turn her head, relieved when she was able to do so without causing pain in her neck. Her head ached, but that was to be expected since she' hit it hard enough to lacerate it. She carefully took inventory as she moved from her neck down, grimacing in pain when she reached her legs. Her left ankle was throbbing in time with her heartbeat. It was crumpled beneath her, and the pain centered around her knee for the moment. She gingerly rolled herself over to her right side, slowly untangling her left leg until it was mostly straight. It didn't want to cooperate, almost as if the top and bottom halves were no longer connected.

Stabbing pain in her knee told her she wasn't walking out of here on her own.

She could still wiggle her toes, and based upon the location of the pain, she guessed she'd done significant damage to the ligaments holding her knee together. She gritted her teeth, and pushed herself up to a sitting position. She was about half a mile from the overhang where she was supposed to meet her hiking partners, and she hoped they had listened to her instructions and headed down the mountain when she hadn't shown up.

Her pack had come off, and she scooted along the wet ground until she could reach it. She pulled her cell phone out, hoping for at least one bar of service. "Please, God." She pointed it in all directions, but still came up with nothing. She wasn't far enough around the side of the mountain yet.

It was snowing harder now, and for the first time in her life, Gracie began to panic. *Pull it together, Grace. You know these mountains. Think. There has to be someplace you can hole up until morning.*

The thought of spending the night, alone and cold, on the face of the mountain was daunting, but Gracie was a fighter. She unzipped her pack, and pulled the thermal blanket from its zipper pouch. She wrapped it around her shoulders, hoping to stave off getting any wetter while she examined her options.

She was sitting at the base of the rock wall, no shelter in site. If she could make it down the mountain another twenty yards or so, she could at least take shelter in the trees and the pine needles. She'd never had a chance to use the survival skills they'd learned in seventh grade science, but suddenly pieces of information popped into her head.

Find shelter from the wind and moisture. The trees would have to do.

Stay someplace where you could be seen from the air by a search and rescue plane. That one was a little more difficult. There was no open space close, but Gracie's jacket was bright red and purple. That should count for something.

Snow caves can save your life. Okay, there wasn't enough snow to build a snow cave, but the idea was that one could use nature to conserve body heat. There was a deep bed of pine needles beneath the trees. She only hoped that it was cold enough that any bugs who'd inhabited the needles during the warmer months had died or were in hibernation. She wasn't a prissy girl who screamed at the sight of a spider, but she also didn't feel up to sharing her makeshift bed with them.

She put her pack on her front, slipping her arms through the straps and tightening them so she wouldn't have to worry about it falling off. She needed all of her concentration for what was to come. She scooted over to the rock wall so that she could try to pull herself to a standing position. It took her several attempts, but she finally was able to use her good leg to push her body up along the rock surface. She was panting with her efforts afterwards, and she stayed there for several minutes to let her head stop spinning and the nausea in her stomach ease. Her knee was protesting the slightest movement vehemently, but she pressed onward.

Ten minutes later, she felt able to continue. She brushed the snow off her hair, and took a look at her goal. The trees to be more specific. She had all of her weight resting on her good leg, and she was trying to ignore the pulsing pain in her injured knee. She just needed to reach the trees. She edged her way along the rock wall, using it as a support beam for as long as possible. When it was time to step out and head for the trees, she gingerly placed some weight on her left leg, screaming in pain as it buckled and she fell forward to the ground. She lay there panting, trying to control the pain, all while refusing to give in to the tears of despair and frustration that were stinging her eyes. "Come on, Grace! You have to do this!"

She pushed her torso up, and slowly began to crawl across the now snow-covered ground, using her good leg to push herself up while her injured leg simply dragged along. Her injured leg felt every stick, rock, and bump along the way, but Gracie gritted her teeth and pressed on.

She felt rocks and debris poke through her gloves, but she didn't stop. If she stayed out in the open, it would possibly be the last thing she ever did. If she reached the trees, hopefully someone would come looking for her soon. If not tonight, then at first light. Her vision was blurry, and her arms felt leaden, but still she moved forward.

It was small comfort given her present predicament, but it was all she had. Determination had gotten her far, and it would see her through this situation as well. It took her twenty minutes before she reached the dense trees. Tears were streaming down her face, freezing before they could drop to the ground and mud and debris covered most of her body.

She lay there, panting with her efforts, trying to take shallow breaths so the nausea would abate. She rolled to her back, and then leveraged herself up under the first tree she came to that was still relatively dry underneath. Her thermal blanket was now covered in mud and melting snow, but she wrapped it around herself anyway. She tried to bend her knee to keep her body heat in close, but the muscles had finally stiffened up to the point that she couldn't even bend it the slightest bit.

She scooped pine needles over her leg, hoping the survivalist who had taught their class actually had known what he was talking about. She wrapped the thin thermal blanket tighter around herself, covering her head and praying for morning to come quickly.

The wind howled, the snow continued to fall, and Gracie finally allowed the exhaustion and pain to overtake her, forcing her body into a deep sleep as her body temperature started to drop.

*****

Mason was sick with worry.

He and Kaillar had found two of the women an hour and a half ago, huddled beneath a rocky overhang, just where Gracie had told them to seek shelter. They were scared and cold, but otherwise in good health. They'd been relieved to see the two men, and then expressed feelings of guilt for not having attempted to make it down the trail on their own.

Neither woman seemed to have enough hiking experience to be up on the mountain in bad weather. Mason had assured them that staying put was actually the best choice they could have made. But they'd been worried sick about their friend. Gracie Shelton.

She was missing, and Mason and Kaillar felt horrible confirming that she had never made a phone call to the ranger station for help. Mason sent Kaillar back down to the station with the other two women, and he pulled a map from his pocket.

The women had described the location where Gracie tried to climb down, and he decided to take an approach from the bottom up. The snow was already an inch thick in most places, and more was accumulating by the minute. Even with ropes and anchors, trying to scale a rock wall in this weather was suicide.

He carefully made his way around the western side of the mountain, using the known trails and avoiding the rockslide areas, as they were too slippery and dangerous in this weather.

He finally reached the rock wall that he assumed Gracie had attempted to climb down, looked up, and shook his head. In this weather, he would have trouble descending this particular wall, and he was an expert climber. *I wonder if she actually scaled the wall, and where she learned to do something this difficult.*

He looked around the ground, and would have missed the signs that someone had been there if he hadn't started to slip and reached out to catch himself. His hand came away from the rock with fresh blood smeared across it.

He looked around frantically trying to see through the falling snow. Cupping his hands around his mouth, he called out, "Gracie!" He sent up a silent prayer, hoping the blood was hers and at the same time, hoping it wasn't. "Gracie! If you can hear me, call out."

He listened carefully, the wind making it difficult to hear. He searched the ground for further evidence, and took his eyes in an ever increasingly wide circle out from the rock wall. When he was almost thirty yards out, he found what he'd been looking for. Drag marks!

He went in that direction, cupping his hands to concentrate his voice, "Gracie!"

He followed the drag marks, and then he saw the shiny silver blanket, partially covered in snow, but covering what appeared to be a very still form.

He slid down the remaining feet, and then quickly brushed the snow off the huddled figure. He pulled the thermal blanket open to reveal a mud covered female he could only assume was the girl of his dreams? *This can't be right. In my dreams, Gracie and I were always re-united in prom attire! Crazy dreams of a teenager, and this is most definitely a full grown woman.*

Shaking his head at the fanciful ideas racing through it, he pulled off one glove and searched for a pulse. It was faint, and her skin was cool to the touch. Too cool. He immediately began to worry about hypothermia.

He shook her shoulder, "Gracie!" He didn't even consider that the woman wasn't Gracie. She bore the same half-moon scar over her right eyebrow as Gracie. A scar she'd received when they'd slipped past the safety gates and gone exploring inside the Silver Springs Mine. They'd been foolish, but at the age of twelve, they'd thought themselves invincible. With the images from the most recent

Raiders of the Lost Ark playing in their heads, they been searching for buried treasure and adventure.

When Justin had realized where they were, they'd hurried to exit the mine before he reached them and had proof of their foolishness, but Gracie hadn't ducked far enough and the metal bolt sticking out of the safety gate had caught her just above the eye.

Doc had taken one looked at her and silently stitched her up before asking how she'd hurt herself. When a tearful Mason had tried to explain, Doc had given both of them a lecture on the dangers of closed up mines, and threatened to tell his uncle and her father if they ever did anything so stupid again.

A gust of wind forced his mind back to the present. He moved her hair back, and that's when he saw the cut and large bump on her forehead. Blood had dripped down the other side of her forehead, but seemed to have mostly stopped now. "Sugar, what did you do to yourself?" He was stunned at the depth of feeling that pulsed through him. He wanted to gather her close to his chest and protect her from all harm. But first, he needed to figure out how she was hurt and find them some shelter.

She wasn't responding to him, and he didn't feel that they had time to waste. He pulled his radio from his pocket and waited until Justin came on. "Mason's on his way to the ranger station with two of the women. The other one tried to climb down the cut wall to call for help. It looks like she fell and cracked her head pretty good."

While speaking, Mason had been moving the leaves she'd piled up around her, pausing when he saw the angle of her extended leg. "She's got some sort of leg injury and a small cut on her head. How about sending the chopper up here?"

"Mason, I wish I could. Visibility is awful, and they just shut down the closest airports."

"Chopper?" Mason asked, already knowing the answer.

"Not until the visibility clears up. How far up are you?" Justin asked.

"About ten thousand feet would be my guess. It's already dumped a few inches in the last half hour. She can't walk down, and I can't carry her that far. Too steep."

"Can you get her down to one of the line shacks?"

Mason thought for a moment and then smiled, "I'd forgotten about those. Yeah, I think I can get her down that far. We should be directly above the closest one."

"That's what I would do. If you can get her some place dry for the night, I'll send someone up to get you just as soon as the storm clears."

"Will do. I'll check in once we reach the shack." Mason pocketed the radio, and then stuffed her thermal blanket back into her pack. They had about a half hour of sunlight, and they needed to be close to the shack before night fell. It was time to put himself to the test. Both of their lives depended upon it.

Chapter 4

Mason made it to the line shack and kicked the door open. Gracie hadn't stirred during their slippery walk down the side of the mountain. He was grateful for that fact, as he'd not been able to carry her through the trees without adding some bumps and bruises to her body.

He laid her down on the floor, and quickly shut the door. It appeared that this shack had been used during the summer as a fresh supply of firewood was in the carrier and someone had taken the liberty of stacking some in the hearth. A stack of old newspapers lay nearby, and he wadded some up and stuffed then beneath the logs before lighting them.

Once he was sure that the fire was going, he took a survey of their surroundings, finding several wind-up lamps and two oil ones. He lit them all, placing them around the single room shack to provide as much light as possible.

Turning back to Gracie, he could see her body shivering as it attempted to maintain her body temperature. He removed her boots, pulled her jacket from her body, and then her jeans, being careful not to disturb her injured leg any more than necessary. She had full thermal underwear on beneath, and he tried to ignore the way his body appreciated her lithe form. She was beautiful, but right now, she was out cold and Mason was growing more worried with each passing minute.

He pulled out a gallon of water from one of the shelves, and used it to wet some paper towels. He carefully wiped her hands and face off, carefully cleansing around the cut on her forehead and wishing they had the benefit of a medical exam. The purplish bruising and swelling was significant, but it was the fact that she was unconscious which worried him most.

He located the sleeping bags, and after shaking them out to make sure they didn't have any uninvited guests, he spread two of them out on the floor in front of the fire. He picked her up, laid her on the sleeping bag, and then opened up another one and covered her with it. He removed his own boots and outerwear, and then sat down next to her.

He let his eyes travel over her still face, seeing the girl she'd been in the woman she'd become. She was gorgeous, her hair was tangled with dirt, leaves, and he thought about trying to comb it out, but just then she started to stir.

Gracie came awake to the feeling of warmth on her face, but her back was freezing cold. She attempted to switch positions, but her leg wouldn't move and the more she struggled, the more pain she felt.

"Easy there, Grace," Mason called to her, laying a gentle hand on her shoulder to keep her in place. "You've injured your knee, but I can't tell how badly..."

"The ACL is tore," she murmured, opening her eyes and gazing up into the face of the man who was both familiar and a stranger to her. She opened her eyes more fully, and took in her surroundings. They were in some sort of cabin, and while it didn't look very sophisticated, it was dry and the heat from the fire was miraculous, considering she'd thought she was going to freeze to death.

"Mason?" she murmured, wanting to make sure she wasn't just imagining him.

"Yeah, sugar. It's me. I almost didn't recognize you. You've changed quite a bit since I last saw you."

Gracie gave him a half smile, "You haven't seen me for eight years. You've changed as well." *But not so much that I didn't immediately recognize you. Still the same little scar on his chin from pretend sword fighting with Kaillar when you were eight. The same dark blue eyes that seemed to see right into her very soul. The hair that always looked like it needed a good combing.*

"You cut your hair," Mason murmured.

Gracie reached up a hand and touched her short strands, "Medical school was tough enough without having to take care of my hair thirty minutes a day."

Growing up, Gracie had never cut her hair. When she'd left Silver Springs, it had reached to just below her waist. She'd loved her long hair, but after getting into medical school, it became a hindrance she didn't need. She'd donated the long locks to a local cancer society that used donated human hair to make wigs for cancer patients.

"Medical school? I heard a rumor that you were talking to Doc Matthews." He watched her carefully, wanting the rumor to be true.

Gracie nodded her head and then winced, "Ouch!"

"You bumped your head pretty good back there. What were you thinking, trying to scale down the cut wall in a snow storm?" Mason allowed just a hint of anger to creep into his voice.

Gracie blushed, "Firstly, it wasn't snowing when I started down. Secondly, I'm an experienced climber. That wall should have been a piece of cake, but I didn't think about there being ice in the crevices. Free climbing isn't my forte, I'll admit, but if I hadn't lost my grip on a crevice full of ice, I would have been fine."

"You're lucky I found you."

"I know that. My friends…"

"Your friends are fine. Kaillar took them back down to the ranger station, and then was going to make sure they arrived at Sarah's safe and sound."

Gracie relaxed and shut her eyes for a moment, the effort of staying awake causing her head to throb painfully. "Thank God. I really was trying to help. They didn't understand the danger of getting caught on the mountain in a snowstorm, and I was hoping to call for help while they took the easier route down. I thought if I could get someone to come up and help us, we could all get down before the storm descended on the mountain."

"That didn't quite work out like you planned it. Did it?" Mason asked, no judgment in his voice.

Gracie looked at him, "What were you doing up on the mountain?"

"My brothers and I are the search and rescue first responders for the county."

"Your brothers are all still in Silver Springs?" she asked in surprise.

"Yeah."

"What about your uncle?" she asked. She'd always liked their Uncle Jed, and he'd always treated her with the utmost respect, and had expected his nephews to do the same. It was one of the first differences between Mason and other boys she'd noticed upon leaving Silver Springs. Mason had always treated her as a lady, and never did anything that could be considered rude or vulgar around her. At med school, she'd met plenty of guys who didn't care that she was a female. They'd engaged in vulgarity just to see her reaction, something she'd been hoping would go away once she got out of high school. It had been her experience that many boys never grew out of that particular character defect.

"My uncle passed away a few years ago," he told her softly.

Gracie felt tears spring to her eyes, "I'm sorry. I know he was very close to all of you."

Mason nodded and then he asked, "What about your parents?"

Gracie swallowed and looked away for a moment. *How do I tell him about my dad and his mom?* She knew that no one in Silver Springs was aware of what had transpired. Part of her wanted to tell him what she knew so that there would be no secrets between them going forward. Another part of her wanted to forget that she knew anything – but ignorance wasn't bliss. As she'd so clearly found out in her own life.

"My dad died a little while ago. My mom is travelling with a group of her friends on a cruise around the world."

"Wow! I'm sorry to hear about your dad. He never did seem to like me much."

Gracie chose to say nothing, not wanting to lie to him. Her father hadn't really liked any of the teenagers in the area. The Donnelly boys had just had the misfortune of being their mother's children, making them even less likable to her father.

Changing the subject, she looked at her surroundings and asked, "So, where are we?"

Mason gave her a look. He appeared to be watching her for panic or something else. She wasn't sure, but before she could ask, he told her, "One of the line shacks on the mountain. They're mostly used by the sheep herders during the summer months, but also by hikers and others who miscalculate and get stuck on the mountain overnight."

"Does anyone know where we are?" she asked, just starting to realize the peril she'd been in.

"I spoke to Justin a bit ago. He knows where we are, and he'll send a chopper for us as soon as the storm clears out."

"Tomorrow?" Gracie asked, her knee starting to talk to her quite loudly. Her head was pounding and the nausea had returned. She didn't want to complain, but she felt horrible.

Mason watched her and then shrugged, "I'm not going to lie to you. Maybe. How's the leg?"

Gracie gave a rough laugh, "To be honest, it hurts. Bad."

"I brought along a first aid kit. Want to take a look, and see if there's anything in there you can use?"

Gracie nodded her head, "Please." Even some over-the-counter pain medication would give her a small amount of relief. "I hate to ask, and actually, can't believe I'm saying this, but is there something around here that could be used as an ice pack?"

Mason chuckled, "Yeah, I can't believe you asked that either. I'll find you something, and there's more than enough snow out there to keep you in ice packs all night long."

Chapter 5

Mason found an empty plastic bag, and stepped outside to fill it with fresh snow. He also grabbed the first aid kit from his pack by the door. He took an extra moment, and looked up at the cloudy sky. "Thank you for helping me to find her."

Mason had gotten them down to the line shack in record time, and then called Justin to give him an update. It was the best he could do for her at the moment, and he was more relieved than he cared to admit that she'd regained consciousness.

Filling the bag with fresh snow, he stepped back inside the shack and shut the door, barring the wind from coming inside.

He walked over to her, gently moved the blanket lying over her legs, and laid the makeshift ice bag on her knee, "That should help some."

"Thanks." Gracie blushed, having just realized that someone had removed her outer clothing. Since there was no one else around, she knew that someone had to be Mason. She'd taken a closer look at her surroundings while he'd been getting the snow, and she'd easily identified her clothing lying in a pile a short distance away. It was caked with mud and very wet.

"I've got some over-the-counter painkillers if you think they might help?" he offered, opening up the first aid kit and pulling out two different bottles. He handed them to her and after she made her choice, he pulled his pack over and pulled out a canteen of water. "Here, this should help wash those down."

"You're a regular Boy Scout, aren't you?" Gracie asked, thankful for everything he did have.

"That's me. I even have a few protein bars and some freeze-dried soup." He didn't have to tell her that Silver Springs had never had a Boy Scout Troop while they were growing up; she knew that.

"Freeze-dried soup?" Gracie asked. "Explain to me how that is supposed to work."

Mason smiled, "I'll go one better and fix us both some." He rummaged through his pack again and came out with a small tin container, two foil packages, and his water canteen. He poured some water into the tin and then set it near the fire. He kept an eye on Gracie as he got the packages ready for the water, not liking how pale her face was; or the fact that she seemed to be having trouble keeping her eyes open.

"Hey, you still with me?" he asked softly, watching her eyes flutter open as she turned her head to look at him. She gave him a small smile, and he grinned back, "You wouldn't want to miss this culinary delight I'm cooking up."

Gracie pushed herself up a bit, so that she was sitting, rather than lying down, grimacing at the new pains that made themselves known. "Did you ever learn to cook?"

Mason grinned, "You still remember Home Ec, huh?"

Gracie grinned, "I don't think any of us will ever forget how you almost burned down the school. Mrs. Peterson even retired at the end of the school year."

"Not because of me," Mason reminded her, remembering how everyone had teased him about being the reason the matriarch of the middle school had decided to move to Florida and play golf, rather than try to teach pre-adolescent boys how to work an oven.

Gracie nodded, "I'm just teasing you. So, I imagine lots of things have changed in Silver Springs?"

Mason grabbed a glove and added some of the hot water to each foil package, using a plastic spoon to stir them up before folding over the tops. "They just need to sit for five or so minutes, and they'll be ready to eat. And, some things have changed, but not as many as you might think."

Mason watched her face and then stated, "Are you seriously considering taking over Doc's practice?"

Gracie nodded, "Yeah, I am. I've always wanted to return, and now that I don't have to fight my dad, I'm really thinking about doing what I want to do."

Fight her dad? What's that mean? Mason didn't ask the question, but echoed her statement, "Coming to live in Silver Springs is what you want to do?"

Gracie nodded, "It is." There were so many things she wanted to ask. And say, but the version of Mason sitting across from her was one she didn't really know. She didn't want to assume he was still the same as the fourteen year old boy who'd given her the first romantic kiss of her life. The same boy she'd swore she loved, and that they would be together forever. They'd been young, and after her father had uprooted his family and moved them away from Silver Springs, everyone had assumed she would forget all about him. But she hadn't.

All through high school and then college, she'd compared every boy who asked her out to Mason. None of them were ever able to measure up, so she'd finally just given up on having a social life that included dating a member of the opposite sex.

She'd thrown herself into her studies, joined a few service organizations, and put finding love on the back burner. Her heart had been given to Mason, and when she'd first thought about returning to Silver Springs, she'd found a hope that somewhere, she might find her heart there as well as her future.

*****

"I'm heading down to Sarah's, do you want to come along?" Justin asked Jessica. Kaillar had called in a few minutes earlier to say that the two women hikers were safely ensconced at Sarah's and seemed to be suffering no lasting effects. At least, not physical ones.

"No, I'm good right here where it's warm. Want me to make dinner while you're gone?" Jessica asked.

Justin smiled and then quickly shook his head, "No, I'll throw a pot of chili together when I get back. Won't take that long to heat through and dinner will be ready." By Jessica's own admission, she couldn't boil water without burning it. There was no way Justin wanted her using the lodge's gas stove with nobody around to put out the fire.

"Are you sure?" She gave him a look that was part teasing and part relief.

"Positive. I'll be back with Kai in a bit." He kissed her on the forehead, feeling blessed to have her in his life. He knew that she still had things to work out, most of them between God and herself, but for the first time, he really felt positive that they had a future together.

Justin headed down the mountain, using the alone time to thank God for helping Jessica deal with her lack of faith. Seeing her walk into the church this morning had been like Christmas come early. "Guess I have a lot of things to be thankful for this week."

He arrived at Sarah's, and found Kaillar speaking with one of the women named Melanie. The other woman was sitting near a window, her arms wrapped around herself in a self-protective gesture, as she watched the snow fall outside.

"She okay?" he asked Sarah quietly.

"Don't know the answer to that one yet. The friend said she's doing okay now, but I guess she started to slip on their way down, and Kaillar caught her. She freaked out; acting completely terrified, and has been withdrawn and quiet since they got here."

Justin watched her for another moment, and then joined Kaillar and Melanie. After the introductions were made, Justin asked Melanie, "What's up with your friend?"

Melanie looked at Becca with compassion in her eyes and smiled sadly, "She was attacked a while back, and I think when your brother grabbed her to stop her fall, it was just similar enough to her attack that it caused all of those old feelings of terror to rise to the surface. She's never dealt with them in my opinion, and it was just a matter of time before something like this triggered a bad reaction."

Seeing how concerned the brothers were, she hurried to assure them, "Don't worry. When Gracie gets here, she'll know what to do, and can medicate her if necessary. She's had to talk her down before."

"Talk her down?" he queried, his eyes on the young woman who seemed to be trying to make herself as small as possible.

"She gets panic attacks sometimes. I think she'd get caught up in her head. Starts making things out to be more than they are, and then they spiral out of control."

Justin shared a look with Kaillar and then turned to address Melanie. "What happens if Gracie doesn't talk her down?"

Melanie's face stiffened, "The last time she had an attack, they had to take her to the ER and put her under. She woke up, tied to the rails of the bed, and under a seventy-two hour psychiatric hold. She's not crazy, just hurting. Gracie will make it all better, though."

Justin cleared his throat and told her quietly, "She's not coming down off the mountain tonight."

Chapter 6

Justin wished he had better news, but he didn't. Plunging ahead, he told her, "Gracie injured her knee, and is going to need a chopper or medivac whenever this storm clears."

"Rats!" Melanie looked at her friend and then asked, "Is there a way for her to talk to Gracie tonight? Maybe that would be enough to keep her from imploding."

Justin looked at Kaillar and shrugged, "We could try the radio from down here. Not sure if the signal is strong enough, but it couldn't hurt."

Kaillar nodded and then grabbed the radio from Justin, "Let me, since it seems I'm the reason she's shut down. I was only trying to help."

Kaillar slowly approached the young woman, trying not to notice her strawberry blonde hair, or the little pixie face that looked so sad and alone. He had the strangest urge to wrap her in his arms and protect her, but he pushed it away. Touching her was the last thing she needed.

"Hey, Becca? I was wondering if you might want to talk to your friend for a minute or two. It seems that Gracie hurt her knee in a fall, and isn't going to make it back down the mountain tonight."

"What?! But she has to come back down. It's too dangerous up there, she'll freeze to death and then…"

"Whoa!" Kaillar held up his hands, stalling her from rising from the chair. "Becca, my brother's with her and they're inside one of the line shacks. They're warm and dry and out of the elements. When the storm clears, we'll fly up and get them. Now, would you like to talk to her?"

Becca slowly nodded her head, and then watched with wide eyes as Kaillar turned the radio on, "Hey, Mason! You copy?"

"Kaillar? Your signal's not very strong. What's up?"

"One of Gracie's friends needs to speak to her for a minute. Is she able to talk?"

"Sure. Just a minute."

"Becca?" Gracie's voice came through the radio loud and clear a few seconds later.

Silent tears streamed down Becca's face, "Gracie, are you all right?"

"Hey, you're crying. I can tell. I twisted my knee a bit, but I'm fine. Mason found me."

"Mason? Isn't he the boy you…"

"Yes, that's the one. Are you and Melanie doing okay?"

"We're at Sarah's. She's really nice. Melanie's husband is coming to get her tomorrow morning."

"I'm sure she's happy about that. What did you think about Kaillar? Have you met Justin yet?"

"Is he the other brother?"

"Yeah. You'll like them all once you get to know them."

Mason listened to the conversation, his eyes never leaving Becca's face. She wasn't arguing with Gracie, but her expression said that getting to know him or his brother was the last thing on her list of things to do.

"What about you? Are you going to be okay until I get back there? I may have to have surgery on my knee to fix it. I think it's torn."

"Uhm…I need to get back home…Surgery…what…"

"Becca, slow down now and breathe with me. Come on. One, in. Two, out. Keep going. One, in. Two, out."

The sounds of Becca breathing and Gracie counting ensued for several more minutes before Gracie lowered her voice, "Better?"

"Yes. Thanks."

"Good. Look, I don't want you trying to get back by yourself. I'd say borrow my car, but the keys are up here with me. Can you stick it out until I can get them to you? You can take my car back to Denver. I won't be driving it until my knee heels."

"Gracie...are you really going to be okay?"

"Yeah. I am." There was a brief pause and then Gracie asked, "Can I talk to Melanie for a minute?"

Becca silently nodded and handed the radio back to Kaillar. She made sure their hands didn't touch, and she refused to meet his eyes. Kaillar was more worried about her now than before. She seemed to have shut down before his eyes while talking to her friend. The exact opposite reaction the phone call was to have had.

"Gracie wants to talk to you," he told Melanie, handing her the radio.

"Gracie?"

"Hey, Mel. What's up with Becca?"

Melanie briefly explained what had happened on the way down the mountain. "She's losing it, Grace. Completely shutting everyone and everything out."

"I wish I was there to help. You need to get her to sleep. Can Michael stick around until I get off this mountain? I don't want her left alone."

Melanie smiled, "Your compassion is what makes you the perfect person to be a doctor. Yeah, Michael's debriefing ended early. He's officially out as of today. He was going to drive over and surprise us anyway. Now he's just coming in without the element of surprise."

"I'm happy for you. See if you can get Becca to get some sleep tonight."

"I will. Justin offered to call the doctor if you think it would help?"

"Only if he'll give her some sleeping medication. She needs to break the cycle of terror her mind is caught up in right now. But just going to sleep might only make it worse. She needs to sleep so deeply that her mind has to turn off for a bit."

Justin gestured for the radio and Melanie handed it to him, "Gracie, its Justin."

"Hi Justin."

"Hey, I'll call Doc myself. Do you have a recommendation for what might help her?"

Gracie rattled off two different sleeping medications she'd used on Becca before when she was like this, and she even gave him the dosages she would recommend if she were there. "Don't forget that Doc has a lot more experience than I do. If he suggests something else or a different dosage, follow his instructions, not mine."

"Are you sure? I mean, you know Becca better than he will."

"I'm sure. I trust Doc to make the right decisions." Gracie sounded confident, and that was good enough for Justin.

"Okay. I'm on it. You and Mason doing okay up there?"

"Just dandy .He just made me freeze-dried soup, and I can't believe I'm saying this, but it wasn't half bad. Not something I'd want to eat on a regular basis, but not bad."

"Good to hear it. Tell Mason we'll be up as soon as we can. Right now, the storm seems to have stalled over the mountains, and doesn't look like it's going to be moving on anytime soon."

"He's right here and heard you. Thanks for taking care of my friends."

"No problem. Talk to you guys soon. Be safe."

Justin turned the radio off, and called the doctor. After explaining to him about the incident on the hike down and Becca's reaction, he also told Doc about Gracie's recommendations. Doctor Matthews seemed impressed with her recommended treatment, and promised to get the prescription filled and bring it by Sarah's in the next half hour.

Meanwhile, Justin and Kaillar could head on up the mountain. He'd check on her when he delivered the sleeping medication, and then Sarah and Melanie could take turns sitting with Becca until she fell asleep.

With a plan in place, Justin and Kaillar headed home, with Sarah promising to call if she needed help of any kind. Melanie's husband was en route, but with the storm, it would be hours before he arrived.

Sarah promised, and Melanie thanked Kaillar again for coming to their rescue. The two brothers headed out, making their way back up the mountain through the ever deepening snow. Justin could tell that Kaillar's mind was still on the frightened woman, and he hoped that they'd have a chance to meet one another when she wasn't quite so terrified. She seemed like a sweet kid, and Justin had seen the look on Kaillar's face. There was more than a passing interest there.

Justin wasn't sure if it was her vulnerability, or how fragile she seemed, that had sparked Kaillar's interest. Growing up, Kaillar had always had a soft spot for those in need. He always championed the underdog, and he tended to be the good looking guy who asked the mousy secretary type out because no one else would.

He'd had plenty of chances to find a girlfriend while working at the local ski resorts. Justin had seen him flirt with the snow bunnies, and yet, he never let the interaction go beyond the ski slopes. It had been the same way in high school. Kaillar had been more interested in playing football than girls, and Uncle Jed had fostered that situation as much as possible.

Now that Kaillar was an adult, Justin knew that he'd been feeling the same pull to settle down and find a wife. To raise some kids. But so far, Kaillar hadn't shown more than a passing interest in anyone he'd met. Until now.

Something about the woman with the pixie face and sad, bruised eyes had gotten to him.

Chapter 7

Monday morning....

Gracie woke up, stretching inside her sleeping bag as she listened for signs of the storm outside. The wind had continued throughout the night, and she and Mason had done their best to stay warm and not worry about how they were going to get back down the mountain in the morning. Mason had continued to feed the fire throughout the night, and she made a mental note to thank him.

They didn't have any cell phone service on this side of the mountain, but they still had the radio, and Mason confirmed that they were only about a mile from the position where he and Kaillar had found her friends.

Gracie tried to shift around, her body clamoring for her to get up and take care of nature's call, but each time she tried to move her leg, the pain in her knee stole her breath away.

"Hey! You doing okay?" Mason asked softly, wanting to let her know he was awake and yet not startle her.

Gracie turned her head and looked at him with a half-smile. "Morning. Did the storm stop?"

"I think so. To tell you the truth, I'm almost afraid to look outside. You girls sure didn't plan this trip out very well, did you?"

"That's my fault, I guess. Although Melanie and Becca were already planning to come up here regardless. I simply asked to tag along, and then ended up driving us here. I should have checked the weather myself instead of relying on one of them to do it."

"Well, don't beat yourself up about it. The mountain seems to have already done a credible job of that." Mason slipped from his sleeping bag, the ultra-low-temperature bags having been part of the accommodations they found in the line shack.

He squatted down next to her, and then checked her forehead, "Hurt?"

"Just a bit. Uhm…well, I hate to ask, but is there any way you could…"

"Don't say another word." Mason scooped her up from the sleeping bag, after unzipping it and assuring himself she wouldn't freeze by spending a few minutes outside in the cold.

He carried her to the door of the shack and then nodded, "Open that, will you? My hands are full at the moment."

Gracie couldn't help but smile in the face of his silliness. She tried not to notice how right it felt to be in his arms. Or how little tingles of reaction shivered up and down her spine. Or how nice he smelled…*Girl, get your head back in the game here. Survival. That's where your brain should be. Oh, and …*

Mason carried her a short distance away from the shack and then propped her up against a tree. "Hang on a second," he urged her, using his booted feet to scrape the majority of the snow away from the base of the tree.

"Just hold onto the tree for balance. When you're finished, holler out and I'll come get you. Do you need anything else?" he asked, shoving some tissues into her hand.

Gracie blushed and shook her head, embarrassed beyond imagination. Mason took himself back towards the shack, and Gracie answered nature's call as quickly as possible.

She tried to reason with herself that this was a simple bodily function, but her modesty and sense of propriety wasn't buying it. *Come on, you dealt with more embarrassing situations in med school. This is nothing. Only what you make of it.*

She finished her business, and then righted her clothing once more. "Mason?" she called out more softly than she intended.

"Right here, sugar. Ready to get back inside and out of the cold?"

She tried not to think about how much she liked his use of the endearments. They made her feel special. Cared for. Dare she say loved?

Gracie nodded and tried to take a step towards him, but the pain in her knee when she put the faintest amount of pressure on it was staggering and swift.

"Ow!"

"Hang on, there girl. Let me carry you back inside." He scooped her up for the second time that day, and Gracie felt her heart speed up at his closeness.

Mason was a gorgeous man, both inside and out. She hadn't seen him in eight years, and had only been reacquainted with him for twelve hours, but his goodness shone like a beacon in the dark. The Mason she'd fallen in love with as a young teenager still existed. And from what she could see, he'd only perfected with age.

As he carried her back into the shack and settled her on top of the sleeping bag spread out before the fire, she couldn't help but let her eyes wander over his face and shoulders.

"How come you're not married?" she murmured, wishing now that she'd had the guts to ask Sarah about Mason and his brothers.

"Never found anyone I wanted to spend the rest of my life with. No sense in dating someone you know isn't the one. I didn't want to waste my time or my affections. My heart was given away a lot of years ago."

His heart was given away a long time ago? How long ago? Could he mean... Gracie watched him, and then searched his eyes, "How old were you?"

Mason met her eyes and then gave her the only answer he could. The truth. "Fourteen."

Gracie sucked in a breath, unwilling to dare to believe that Mason had felt as strongly about her as she had him. True, they'd promised to be there for each other for the rest of their lives, but they'd been so young. No one had really thought they knew their own minds back then.

Now, eight years later, Gracie found herself trying to adjust to the knowledge that Mason might still have feelings for her. Feelings that might mirror the ones she still held for him? Was it even possible? She had no problem reminding herself how much Mason had meant to her back then, but she'd never in a million years figured that Mason would care the same way still.

Realizing things were headed into waters that she wasn't ready to swim in yet, she looked around and changed the subject. "It looks like something one would find on a Christmas card."

Mason gave her a sidelong look, but then allowed the change of topic. "We got at least a foot of snow last night. And it's mighty wet snow at that. Avalanche danger is going to be high in the backcountry for the next several days."

Gracie nodded, having forgotten how risky wet snow this early in the season could be. "You and your brothers don't..."

Mason shook his head, "No. Not anymore. We did for a while, but there was an accident a few years back where a park ranger guessed incorrectly about the safe zone. He shot the charges to trigger the avalanche, and ended up dying in it. Now, they contract out with professionals."

Gracie felt relieved at that knowledge. She felt a chill as the wind picked up and changed direction. Rubbing her arms for warmth she inquired, "Do you think the chopper is coming sometime today?"

"Justin radioed a few minutes ago. It's already scheduled to be here in a few hours. There's just one little problem. The wind on this side of the mountain is too dangerous and unpredictable for him to land here."

"What does that mean?" Gracie asked, sure she wasn't going to like the answer.

"It means we need to get to a clearing about half a mile from here before he can pick us up safely."

Half a mile? It seemed like an impossible feat in her current condition. "Mason, there's no way I can walk half a mile."

"You won't have to. I have a plan." He looked almost excited at the prospect of putting his plan into action.

"This is really not going to be much fun," she murmured more to herself than the man watching her.

"Are you doubting my ability to get us to our pickup location?"

Gracie looked at him and shook her head, "Not really, just stating the obvious."

Mason grinned at her and then asked, "Remember what we used to do on days right after a big snow?"

Gracie looked at him, realizing where his thoughts were going and immediately started shaking her head with an incredulous laugh. "No! You can't be serious!"

Mason nodded his head, grinning broadly, "Oh yeah! I'm serious. Rest up. I'll be back in a bit."

Chapter 8

"Okay, mademoiselle. Your chariot awaits," Mason told her as he stepped back into the shack almost an hour later. He gave her a bow, and pretended to remove his hat as well.

Gracie chuckled, smiling as pure happiness filled her soul. It seemed like forever since she'd felt this happy inside, and it was all because of the man standing in front of her. "Mason…"

She searched his eyes, wanting to tell him how she was feeling, and yet afraid that she'd misread him and the entire situation. *Maybe it's just being in this place that feels so good.*

"Hey! Don't think so hard. This is going to be fun, and I promise not to go too fast."

Gracie rolled her eyes, "That is so very encouraging, Mario." She used the nickname his brothers had given him one winter when they were ten, borrowed from a famous race car driver known for his speed – Mario Andretti. Mason loved speed and whether it was a toboggan, an inner tube, or skis – he was reckless and fearless. And Gracie really wasn't sure he'd changed much. The laughter in his eyes was so much like the younger version she remembered, she wouldn't be surprised if they both came to regret what was about to happen.

"Hey!" Mason evidently had seen her doubt and the concern in her eyes. He squatted down and cupped her chin, "I promise to go nice and easy. Slow even." He said the word as if it something horrible, but nodded his head to back up his promise.

Gracie laughed, "Okay, let's go see this chariot you constructed."

Mason stood up, and then scooped her up into his arms. Striding to the open shack door, he stepped out into the morning sunshine, "Tada!"

Gracie looked at the rough litter he'd constructed from fallen limbs he'd scavenged and what looked like a...door? He'd laced the boughs together with a length of rope she assumed he had in his pack, and then padded it with fresh pine boughs. "Wow!"

"Cool, huh?"

"Like I said, a regular Boy Scout." She looked at his creation once more, and then looked at his face, "Just one question, where did you find a door?"

Mason pointed towards the outhouse she hadn't even noticed sitting behind the shack. "I borrowed the door. No one will be using this area until Spring, and I'll personally make sure that the door is returned, or another one is installed before then."

"You made a survival sled out of an outhouse door?" Gracie asked in wonderment as her eyes took in the contraption he'd pieced together.

"Right? I'm a genius, I know. Now, let's see how well it works." He sat her down on top of the pine boughs, and then retrieved both of their packs. He handed hers into her hands and then fiddled around with his much larger one until he produced a pair of snowshoes.

"What are you going to do with those?" she asked, not seeing how they were going to help them sled...she broke off when he also produced two nice smooth pieces of wood which he clipped onto the bottom of the snowshoes. "Ah!"

"Clever, huh? I haven't had the opportunity to play with these as of yet. This should be fun!"

"Mason, I don't know..."

"Trust me."

Trust him? "Well, I would love to, but Doc is really counting on me being alive to take over his practice. Maybe you should go meet the chopper, and bring one of the snow machines back up here, or something…"

Mason had finished strapping the shoes to his feet, and slipped his pack over his shoulders. Taking a few small experimental steps, he grinned when he didn't fall over, but smoothly slid over to where she sat.

"Ready?"

"To die? Sure," Gracie told him, both teasing and silently praying that in this area, Mason had most definitely changed. Rushing headlong down the side of Maroon Peak on top of a makeshift litter was not her idea of a pleasant way to die. Not today anyway.

"Oh ye of little faith!"

Gracie laughed, "Quoting Scripture? Really? Well how about 'Forsake foolishness and live!' That's seems to fit quite nicely."

Mason chuckled, "Proverbs?"

"Words to live by," she added with a smile.

Mason chuckled and then told her with confidence, "This is not foolishness. This is ingenuity at its finest." Without further ado, Mason slipped on his gloves, picked up the long poles on the litter and suggested, "Hang on!"

Gracie grabbed the sides of the litter, emitting a little scream mixed with both joy and fear as the litter began to move forward. She did her best to keep her weight in the middle of the litter so that they wouldn't accidentally tip over. Mason guided the litter over the fresh powdery snow, and as they exited the trees and entered a nice open space, she tipped her head back and met his laughing eyes.

"Okay! This is awesome!"

"Told you so." He made sure to keep their speed down, and soon he could see the chopper circling overhead. "There's our ride!"

Gracie looked up, shielding her eyes from the sun. The chopper circled overhead once, and then it slowly descended to land on the snow a short distance away. Mason stopped their litter, and quickly removed his snowshoes before reaching down for her.

"Ready to go get that knee looked at?" he asked, knowing that she'd been in pain all morning and doing her best to ignore it.

Gracie groaned, "A shower sounds better, but I guess I better go get it checked out."

"Okay. Let's hit Vail first and then if they release you to go today, I'll have Justin or Kaillar drive over and pick us up."

"I don't want to put you guys out any more. You don't have to stay at the hospital with me." *But I really hope you will.*

Her wish seemed to be his as well. Just before they reached the chopper, he stopped and whispered into her ear, "Tell me I'm not the only one who feels like you never left eight years ago."

Gracie searched his eyes and shook her head, "I can't. I feel the same way. This morning…"

Mason kissed her forehead tenderly, "Was just the beginning. Let's get your knee fixed up and then go from there. I'm really glad you came back to Silver Springs."

"So am I." *I wish I'd never had to leave.* She tried not to think about the reasons she'd been forced to leave in the first place. She didn't want to dredge up the past, knowing that nothing other than pain would result. For her. And for the Donnelly brothers. Her father was the impetus that had caused their mother to take off, and the reason she'd never been able to come home again.

Would Mason still have feelings for her once he knew the truth? That was one question that she was in no hurry to get answered.

Chapter 9

Vail Hospital facility, Monday afternoon…

Gracie gave the orthopedic surgeon a small smile as he left the exam room, and then she leaned her head back against the gurney and closed her eyes. *Guess you're going to get a chance to see what being a patient is like, up close and personal.*

She'd been right in her initial assessment that she'd done a number on her ACL- her anterior cruciate ligament. Just a little piece of fibrous tissue, but one that performed the job of connecting the major bones in her leg together. She hadn't torn it completely apart, but the tear was significant enough that without surgical intervention, it most likely would never heal properly.

Dr. Geske was a very well-known orthopedist who just happened to be available to immediately perform the surgery. Since she'd not eaten anything for breakfast due to some nausea, and her head CT had come back clean, she was good to be put under anesthesia right away.

Mason stuck his head around the exam curtain and moments later asked "Hey! Can I come in?"

Gracie scooted herself back up on the bed, her leg completely immobilized by the leg brace a nurse had applied to it upon her arrival. She smiled and waved him forward, "Sure, come on in."

"So I passed Dr. Geske in the hallway, and he said you're headed up to surgery in a few minutes?"

"Yeah." Gracie cleared her throat, and then nodded her head, "The ACL is torn pretty badly. But the good news is that Dr. Geske is here and can fix it today. I'll be in a leg brace for six weeks or so, which will make getting around in the snow interesting, but after that and some therapy, I should be good as new."

"That is good news. Not the surgery or the rehab part, but I'm glad Stan's here to fix things up."

"Stan?" Gracie asked.

"Dr. Geske. He's been courting Sarah for the last several months, but she's pretty adamant about not giving up her place in Silver Springs, and he can't really move too far away from the hospital."

"Do they..."

"Love each other?" When she nodded, he grinned, "Yeah. But Sarah has some misguided notion that if she leaves town, no one will take over the motel and travelers and visitors alike won't have any place to stay. Not everyone wants to drive up the mountain for a night's stay."

Gracie's brain took off running. *Becca would be perfect taking over for Sarah!*

Gracie knew that moving to a small town would be a perfect place for her damaged friend to heal, and Becca knew firsthand how to run a hospitality business. She'd grown up on the Big Island of Hawaii, her parents owning and operating a tourist resort there. Gracie had never understood why a beach girl would leave and move to the mountains of Colorado, and Becca had never gone back home to her knowledge. At least, not in the last four years they'd known one another.

"Hey, where'd you go?" Mason asked, reaching over and clasping her cold hand in his big warm ones.

"I was thinking about Sarah's problem and a solution to it."

"Really? Well, I'm sure Stan would love to hear about it."

Gracie nodded her head, "Once I get out of here, I'll see what I can do. Not sure it will work, but I think I know of just the person to take over Sarah's place so that she can move here."

"Well, why don't you worry about getting yourself better before you try to solve everyone else's problems? I called Justin, and Kaillar's going to drive over tonight. He'll drive us both home in the morning."

"Home?" Gracie murmured, not having given much thought to the logistics once she left the hospital. The surgery would only require an overnight stay, and then only because it was happening so late in the day. They wouldn't let her leave until they were sure that she wasn't going to experience any negative side effects from being put out. They would also want to make sure she had good control of her pain level. Being a physician herself, she would be given more leeway than other patients, but only as much as she could convince Dr. Geske she was going to be a good patient.

"I also spoke with Doc. Now, don't be upset; but I thought he would want an update on your condition. He wasn't expecting you to start until after this week."

"I wasn't planning on it. My trip up here was designed to lock down a place to stay and get the paperwork figured out."

"Well, is there any reason you need to go back to Denver before the weekend?" Mason asked, hoping she would say no.

Gracie thought for a moment and then shook her head, "Not really. My lease on my apartment is up at the end of the month, and Melanie is good to go with her husband now since his discharge is complete."

"What about the other girl? Becca?"

Gracie shook her head, "Becca moved out last month. She's hoping to land a job with the Division of Wildlife as a photographer, and she didn't want to hold Melanie or me up. She's renting on a month to month basis right now."

"So, what about your stuff?"

"Well, I do need to go back and finish packing things up, but with my knee…I don't know how that's going to happen. I might just have to hire some movers…"

"Nonsense. How about you spend Thanksgiving with us at the lodge, and Friday we'll head back to Denver with the truck and the trailer and move you back here?"

Gracie looked up at him and shook her head, "Mason, you don't have to take care of me. I know you must have other things to do…"

Mason sat down on the edge of the bed, keeping her hand in his. He met her eyes and lowered his voice, "Gracie, I feel like the last eight years I've been in a holding pattern. I never forgot you, and while I admit there were days I didn't think about you, I never much looked at another girl. I couldn't. When you left Silver Springs, you took my heart with you. And now you've brought it back."

He stood up and shoved a hand through his hair, "I know this sounds crazy. And I can't explain it, but seeing you again…being with you…I feel like my life can finally start moving forward once again."

Gracie felt tears sting her eyes. No one, not her parents, or even the few friends she'd made in med school, had been able to understand how a boy she'd grown up with and given her heart to as a young teenager could affect her so strongly. They had all accused her of being overdramatic, and living a childhood fantasy.

But Gracie had known, deep in her soul that Mason was the one God had set aside for her. She'd known it then, and she knew it now.

"Mason, you don't have to try and explain it to me. I feel the same way."

"Then it's settled." Mason stopped speaking when a nurse and the anesthesiologist entered the room. "I'll see you on the other side." He winked at her, and then slipped back out of the curtained area.

"So, Miss Shelton. I hear you're going to be our guest for the next few hours. Just a few questions, and then we'll head upstairs…"

Mason headed for the surgery waiting room, praying silently that God would watch over her, and offering up prayers of thankfulness for keeping them safe thus far. Gracie would get her knee fixed and for the first time in years, Mason was actually looking forward to the upcoming holidays. He had much to be thankful for this year.

Chapter 10

Monday evening, Vail Hospital…

Gracie was having the most horrible dream. She was standing on the top of Maroon Peak, the snow was blowing around her, and she was pleading with someone. She looked around her, and there in the distance was her father. She was pleading with her father to undo it. To take back the wrong he'd done, and not destroy all of their lives.

Her mother stood a short distance away, a blank expression on her face as she watched the interaction between her husband and her daughter without emotion.

"Mom! Make him undo it!"

"Dad! Why can't you undo it? Please! At least tell the truth!"

Her father wasn't saying anything. He just stood there, looking resolute. Determined to hide his sin for as long as possible, no matter what the cost to his wife and daughter.

Gracie wasn't a young girl in her dream; she was a grown woman. A grown woman who had allowed his father's actions to destroy her life.

And then her dream shifted, and she was standing at the edge of canyon. Mason stood on the other side, and she walked up and down, trying to find a way across to him. There was no bridge, just the remnants of rope and boards, dangling from the opposite side.

"Mason! Help me!"

Justin and Kaillar joined Mason, and handed him a picture. Mason looked at the picture and then at his brothers. Finally, he looked across the canyon to where she was standing with her arms outstretched.

"Mason! Help me! The bridge is out!"

Mason looked at her with saddened eyes, turning the picture in his hands around so she could see it. It was a picture of his mother. When he looked up at her again, she felt his abandonment clear to her soul. He knew what her father had done, and now wanted nothing to do with her. Nothing...

Gracie jerked awake, a scream of agony lodging in her sore throat. She blinked her eyes to see pale green walls, and the persistent beeping of a machine nearby. She turned her head, and could see the heart rate monitor and pulse oximeter happily running, and then she realized she was in a hospital room. In a hospital bed, to be exact.

The dream was still so vivid in her mind, that when Mason walked in a moment later, she felt tears flood her eyes as she waited for him to leave her a second time.

"Gracie? Sugar, what's wrong? Are you in pain? I can get a nurse," he seemed frantic as he pushed her call button and searched her face. "Hang in there, hon. They'll get you some more pain medications in just a minute."

Gracie shook her head, "No meds." Her voice was hoarse, and she realized it was from the ventilator tube they'd inserted during the operation. Her throat hurt almost as bad as her knee.

Mason gave her a tight smile, "Of course you need more meds. I don't like seeing you hurt."

But you're going to hurt me when you find out the truth. You won't be able to stop it.

Suddenly, Gracie knew that she'd never be able to handle his rejection when it came. *Better to go back to the way things were before she came back to Silver Springs. Better to only grieve a dream, and never know just how perfect her life could have been. If only...*

She looked up at him, and then away. She couldn't do this. Not with him standing there, looking so concerned for her. Loving her? *Heavenly Father, please give me strength...*

She waited for some measure of comfort to fill her soul and mind, but it was as if she'd just asked a brick wall for help. All she felt was helplessness as she contemplated making Mason leave. *Don't send him away. Trust him.* The little voice inside her head was trying to talk sense into the muddled mess of her emotions, still vividly entangled with her dream. Reality and fantasy seemed to blend together, until she could only feel the gaping hurt from her dream.

The nurse entered and misread the situation entirely. "Gracie, I have a stronger painkiller right here. I'm going to put it into your IV so it will kick in faster."

Gracie kept her head turned away until the nurse started to leave and then she reached out and grabbed her hand. She kept her eyes off Mason and then begged the nurse, "Please have him leave."

The nurse looked at her as if she were insane, "Hon? Surely you don't mean that."

Gracie nodded her head, more tears falling from her eyes. "I'm sure." She turned her head away, listening as the nurse, Glenda according to her name badge, explained to Mason that Gracie needed her rest, and that his presence seemed to be upsetting her.

When Mason protested vehemently being asked to leave the room, Gracie's heart broke in two pieces as the nurse told him that her patient had requested he leave.

"Gracie? Sugar, what's going on?"

"Sir, I really must adhere to my patient's wishes. You could leave your name and number at the nurses' desk, just in case she changes her mind."

Gracie could hear Mason arguing with her, begging the nurse to just let him find out what was wrong, but she was a fierce warrior and ushered him from the room with a dire warning to not come back until he was asked.

The nurse stepped back inside the room, handing her a handful of tissues and told her, "Girl, I don't know what craziness is going through your brain, but that man out there loves you. He hasn't left your side except to use the facilities since you came out of surgery. Frankly, he was starting to drive us all crazy with the questions and such."

Glenda came around and sat so that Gracie and she could see each other. "Gracie, hon, you look like your world just crashed down around you. It might help you to get things back into perspective if you could talk about them."

"Talking won't undo what's already been done. I should have never come back to Silver Springs. I just wanted to forget the past and move forward, but I guess deep down I knew that wouldn't be possible. No one can truly move forward if they don't deal with the past first, right?"

Glenda looked at her and then asked, "That depends on whether or not it's your past. Hon, do you believe in God?"

Gracie nodded her head and offered a watery smile, "He's the only reason I've made it this far."

"Good, then you know there's nothing too hard for Him to handle. Let me ask you something. This thing that can't be undone – did you do it?"

Gracie shook her head, "No. And that's what makes it so hard. I didn't even know what had happened until years later. But it robbed that man out there of the chance to grow up knowing his mother. And when he finds out why she ran off and got killed, he's going to blame me."

Glenda was quiet for a long moment and then she asked, "Would you blame you if the roles were reversed?" Glenda asked.

Gracie blinked, once and then again. "I...I guess..."

Glenda stood up and patted her shoulder, "That pain medication is starting to take effect. Do yourself and that young man out there a favor and put yourself in his shoes; figure out how you might react if the roles were reversed. I'll be back later to check on you."

Glenda exited the room to see Mason leaning up against the wall outside; a stricken and confused look on his face. She walked over and stood right in front of him, "Give her some time."

"I don't understand...what's going on here?"

"My guess is she was keeping something from you and the anesthesia caused everything to get all jumbled up in her head. She seems to think she's to blame for your mother's death."

"What?! That's preposterous. My mom died when I was an infant. How could Gracie have had anything to do with that? I need to go talk to her."

Glenda stayed him with a hand on his arm, "I can't let you do that. Look, whatever this incident in her past is, she believes you'll hate her when you find out the truth. My advice to you, stay close and pray that God will help her realize she's not responsible for the actions of another."

"What other? She feels guilty for something someone else did?"

"I believe so. Now, I need to get back to work. Don't give up on her. This may seem like a tsunami, but I've lived long enough to know that true love can weather any storm. That little girl in there wouldn't be so devastated if you didn't already own her heart."

Mason nodded, and watched the nurse walk away. He glanced at the door to her room, and wanted so badly to push it open and demand that she talk to him, but for some reason, she was shutting him out.

He'd seen the hurt in her eyes and the tears. She thought she knew what was best for them both. But he knew a thing or two about doing the right thing, and that was why he walked down to the waiting room and prepared himself for the longest night of his life. A night where he would stand in the gap for her and make sure that if she needed him, he was there for her. He wasn't going to leave. He just got her back, and unlike when they were fourteen and her parents were making all the decisions, he wasn't letting her go without a fight.

Chapter 11

Kaillar arrived at the hospital in Vail, and found a place to park. He'd heard from Mason an hour earlier, and something was definitely wrong. Gracie had made it through her surgery with flying colors, but Mason had sounded off, and his voice was strained.

He asked at the front desk, and was directed to the third floor waiting area. He pushed open the door to see Mason looking much worse for wear.

"Hey! You look awful," he told Mason, taking a seat next to him.

Mason seemed to pull himself together, and took a deep breath, "Did you just get here?"

"Yeah. Why are you sitting in here instead of in there with Gracie?"

Mason was exhausted, and his ability to control his emotions was almost gone. "She kicked me out."

"Were you making a nuisance of yourself?" Kaillar asked, remembering times when all the boys had been sick and Mason had been a pest. He seemed to always recover quickest, and had loved teasing his older brothers, with anything available. Food. Playing outside. Going to town with their uncle.

"No. I mean," he took a breath; "she said she doesn't want to see me. She had the nurse kick me out of the room."

Kai looked at him and then the door leading to the hallway. "And you don't know why?"

Mason shook his head, "I've been sitting here trying to figure out what I did that...Everything was fine before she went into surgery. She was happy. I was happy. Seeing her again…it was as if she'd never left. But now…Kai, she seems to think she's somehow to blame for mom's death."

"Mom? She never knew mom. None of us really did, except for Justin."

"The nurse seems to think she's just confused from the anesthesia, and that she'll come around once her system gets rid of the drug."

"Is that normal? Or even possible?" Kai asked.

"I don't know. How could she think she's responsible for our mother's death? We hardly ever talked about our mother growing up."

Kai nodded his head. The subject of Maria Donnelly rarely came up between the boys. They had all managed to forgive her early on in their lives, and saw no reason to bring her up, or let her have any control whatsoever over their lives. He wasn't about to let the status quo change now. "Let me go try to talk to her," Kai offered.

"Be my guest." Mason didn't expect his brother to make any headway, but he was willing to try anything. He really needed some answers.

Kaillar nodded once, and then headed towards the nurses' station. "Glenda?"

"Yes?"

"Hi. I'm Kaillar Donnelly. I was wondering if I could see Gracie Shelton? I realize it's kind of late, but I just spoke with my brother…"

Glenda nodded, "Room 306. Please be aware that if she pushes her button and asks me to escort you from the room, I won't have any choice but to do so."

"I understand. I don't want to upset her. Gracie, and I go back to when we were kids. We all grew up together."

Glenda smiled and nodded her head towards the door, "Good luck."

Kaillar pushed open the door to Gracie's room and noticed right away that there were no lights on, no television playing, just darkness and the beeping of the machines next to her. He closed the door quietly, and then made his way to the bed.

He didn't want to wake her up, but there was just a sliver of moonlight coming through the windows and he could see her eyes were wide open. "Gracie?" he whispered.

She turned her head and then gave him a sad smile, "Kai."

"Hey, sweetie. I thought you went to medical school to become the doctor, not the patient?"

She smiled and then swallowed painfully, "Water?"

Kai looked around, and spied a pitcher of ice water sitting on the bedside table with an empty glass next to it. He poured the glass half full, and then added a flexible straw to the glass so that she could drink without wearing it.

He held the glass for her, noticing how shaky her hands were. When she was finished, he put the glass down and pulled up a chair. "You feeling any better?"

"Pain's manageable." She paused and then asked, "Where's Mason?"

"Waiting room trying to figure out what he did wrong."

Gracie's eyes filled with fresh tears. "He didn't do anything wrong. None of us did anything wrong, but that …"

"Gracie, hon, you're not making any sense. The nurse told Mason you think you're to blame for our mother's death?"

Gracie nodded, her tears making speech impossible.

"Hon, what do you know about our mother? To my knowledge, we didn't spend any time talking about her while growing up."

"My parents knew her."

"Your parents grew up in Silver Springs, as did my mother and Uncle Jed. So did Sarah and half the town. I would expect all of them to know her. What did they tell you about her?"

"Not they. My dad."

"Your dad told you about my mom?" Kaillar asked, trying to figure out what questions he should be asking, but so far, the conversation didn't appear to be going very far very fast.

"How did your mom die?" Gracie asked in a whisper.

Kaillar sighed, "They aren't really positive, but she was found in a dark alley in Las Vegas. She had drugs and alcohol in her system, and had been beaten up pretty bad."

"I'm so sorry. So sorry." Gracie kept whispering her apology as tears dripped from her eyes.

"Gracie, why are you sorry? Our mother made her own choices. Justin, Mason and I are just thankful that she had the good sense to come home each time she got pregnant with one of us, and that Uncle Jed stepped in to raise us when she couldn't."

"She could have if she'd stayed in Silver Springs."

"She never stayed long in Silver Springs. Gracie, our mother was a druggie and all manner of other things. According to Uncle Jed, she had dreams of becoming famous, and when they fell apart, so did she. She turned to whatever would pay the bills and buy her next fix. I don't know what you think happened, but Maria Donnelly lived for herself and only herself."

Gracie shook her head, "My dad said she was trying to get her act together. After Mason was born, she was trying to stay clean…"

"Yeah, that's what Uncle Jed thought as well. When she left, she cleaned out his bank account, and left him a letter begging him not to come after her. She wanted him to raise her boys, and save them from knowing how badly she'd messed up her life."

"Why did she leave? What caused her to run away?"

"She didn't run away. Running away would mean she at one point intended to stay. Gracie, our mother never wanted to live in Silver Springs, or be a mother, or any of the other things normal people do. She left and went back to her life. Her choice. No one else's."

Gracie wanted so badly to believe what Kaillar was saying, but she'd been afraid of Mason and his brothers finding out what her father had done for so long, she couldn't just let it go. She hadn't fully appreciated how afraid she'd been, but her dream – nightmare really, had brought everything to the forefront of her mind.

The absolute loneliness and hurt she felt when the dream Mason turned away from her was not one she could, or would, soon forget. She saw and felt it each time that she closed her eyes. She knew she'd relive it each time she saw him.

"Gracie, whatever you think you're responsible for, you're not. You were an infant when our mother died. By her bad choices, not those of a baby."

She kept silent, closing her eyes as exhaustion and the pain meds pulled her under.

"Sleep now. And remember that Mason loves you. He's always loved you, and if he has to lose you again, it will destroy him. And, I think it would destroy you as well."

Kaillar left her room, his heart heavy as he tried to figure out what Gracie was so afraid of. And she was afraid. He could see it in her eyes. He stopped by the nurses' station, and met Glenda's eyes, "She's sleeping now."

"Did you get any answers?"

"No, but whatever is bothering her has to do with our mother. I'll go join my brother…"

"Look, she's probably going to be out for most of the night now. Why don't you and your brother head up to the sixth floor. There are some guest suites up there for family members to use when they're here overnight. Get some rest, and hopefully everything will look much better in the morning."

Kaillar thanked her, and went to retrieve his brother. A goodnight's sleep could be used by everyone. Most especially Gracie and Mason. He had a feeling that things were going to get more confusing before they got any better.

Chapter 12

Tuesday late morning...

"Gracie, I would like to see you in ten days to check how things are progressing. You'll need to start physical therapy, but not for at least six more weeks. I know that seems like a long time, but you will need to be your own best patient if you want a full recovery."

Gracie nodded her head, "Yeah. I'll be careful. So," she read over her discharge instructions, "Rest. Ice. Elevation. No weight for six weeks. Got it."

Stan smiled at her, and then folded her chart closed, "I understand that you might have someone in mind to help Sarah manage the motel and boarding rooms in Silver Springs?"

Gracie hadn't even given that another thought; her mind had been occupied with what she was never going to have. "Maybe. I'll have to speak to this person and then if it sounds feasible, I'll have them contact Sarah."

Stan sighed, "If this pans out, it would be an answer to prayer. Sarah has no problems moving over here and marrying me, but she says she won't do it if it's going to leave Silver Springs without proper accommodations."

"I may have been gone for eight years, but that sounds like the Sarah I once knew. After her husband died, I remember that she threw herself into helping at the schools and the church. Anywhere she could put her hands to use, and not sit around bemoaning what she didn't have any longer."

"She's an amazing woman, and I feel blessed just to know her. Even more so to know that she's in my life."

"Congratulations. I'll speak to my friend soon."

"Thanks. One more thing before I take off," Stan told her. "There are two men out there in the hallway, one of whom is hurting because you're hurting." He paused for a moment, and then looked at her with compassion and understanding, "Gracie, whatever is going on in that brain of yours can't be as bad as you think. You've no doubt read about the side effects of anesthesia. Combine those with a deep seated fear, and reality tends to get warped along the way. Talk to Mason. Remember, God didn't create us to go through this life alone."

Gracie nodded, "Thanks. Things don't seem quite so dire as they did yesterday, but that doesn't mean there isn't still going to be hurt feelings…"

"Gracie, do you have feelings for Mason? Before you answer, I know all about you leaving when you were fourteen and the two of you only becoming reacquainted again in the last two days. But Mason seems sure of his feelings. How about you?"

Gracie swallowed and looked out the window before answering, "Have you ever wished you didn't know something?"

"Yes." When she didn't say anything else, he asked, "Is this something what you're afraid of?"

She nodded, not saying anything. He gave her an encouraging smile, letting her know that silence was okay in this instance. "Is this something only you know?"

"And one other living person." *My mother who seems to have gone on living without a care in the world.*

"What have they done with the knowledge?"

Gracie gave a rueful grin, "They forgave and moved on with their life. But the people who don't know, I'm afraid they won't be able to do that. And I will be a constant reminder of what might have been."

"My best advice is to follow your heart. If you have feelings for Mason, you'd be a fool to throw them away. He's one of the good ones." Without another word, he turned and headed for the door. "Oh, and I'm letting him take you home to make sure you follow my discharge instructions."

"But...," Gracie stammered after him, but he walked out of the room and the door closed firmly behind him. She was still staring at the door long moments later, when it opened and Mason stepped in.

She averted her eyes and struggled to keep her composure. She couldn't think of a thing to say to him, but he seemed to realize her trouble, and came to her rescue.

"Stan says you're already to go. Nurse Glenda is bringing up a wheelchair right now." He walked closer to her and then sat down on the edge of the bed so that they were eye level with one another. "Gracie, I don't know what happened yesterday, or what you're not telling me. And if you never want to tell me, that's fine. I don't need to know. If whatever it is causes you this much pain, keep your secret to the grave and I won't ever ask. I just want you to know that no matter what it is, nothing could ever change the way I feel about you. Nothing."

Gracie raised damp eyes to his, "How can you say that when you don't know what it is?"

He smiled at her, "I can say that because I know that no matter what has happened in the past, I can't change a thing. I don't think you could have changed a thing either, and to penalize yourself for the rest of your life doesn't seem fair. I want a relationship with you. I want moonlit walks along the river. Camping trips under the full moon. And I want to see little images of you and me running into my arms at the end of a long day.

"I want the whole package. If you had asked me three days ago if I knew what I wanted for my future, I would have shrugged and told you I hadn't found it yet. Because I wasn't really looking. I think my soul knew that one day you and I would be in the right time and place to make this work. Please, come to the lodge with Kaillar and me for Thanksgiving. Justin is cooking, and he's much better than I am. Give us a chance."

Gracie wanted what he was offering so badly, and since she really didn't have any other options, she slowly nodded her head, "Okay. I'll come to the lodge. Justin's not making freeze-dried turkey is he?"

Mason smiled at her, and slowly shook his head. She felt her heart turn over in her chest, and little butterflies took flight in her stomach. He'd said he didn't need to know her secret. *Could it really be that easy? That she could just not ever tell him and his brothers, and she could pretend that she didn't know anything?*

Somehow, she'd never found anything in life that easy. She was still pondering that when Glenda pushed a wheelchair into the room and shooed Mason out so that she could help Gracie get dressed.

"Came to your senses?" Glenda asked, as she removed her IV and wrapped a piece of pink stretchy tape around her wrist in a pressure bandage.

"Not really, but he says he doesn't need to know what I haven't told him."

"Sounds like a prince among men if you ask me."

Gracie lifted her hips off the bed as the nurse slid a pair of scrub pants up and over the bandaging around her knee. "He's pretty special."

Glenda looked at her and placed her hands on her hips, "Maybe I should get the eye doctor up here before you leave. If you're just seeing that now, girl, maybe you don't deserve him." She fastened the leg brace in place over the scrubs, and then asked, "Too tight?"

Gracie shook her head, and took the scrub top from the nurse, slipping it over her head.

Gracie let those words play over in her head, things that Kaillar and Stan had said replaying in her mind. *Deserve.* The word seemed to be stuck in her head and try as she might, she couldn't get rid of it.

All the way across the mountain and then up to the lodge, she sat silently in the back seat of Kaillar's Range Rover, looking at the mountains and snow, and trying to figure out what she deserved.

She wasn't any closer to figuring things out when they pulled up in front of the lodge than when they'd left Vail. As she looked at the lodge, really looked at it for the first time in years, and all she saw was beauty. The log cabin looked so inviting, and she was suddenly so homesick, she felt tears spring to her eyes.

The two story structure was nestled among the trees, just like when she'd been here last, but there had been significant changes made as well. They had continued the porch all the way around the structure and poured a large patio deck off the side. Rustic log furniture was situated on the deck, and around a large fire pit that rose up from the concrete patio.

Several feet of snow covered all of the unadulterated surfaces, and larger piles of snow were evidence of some shoveling that had occurred earlier in the day. The red metal roof was barely visible beneath the snow, and the splashes of color gave the entire place a festive appearance.

Pine trees, mixed with bare-limbed quaking aspens, had been expertly left in place around the smaller cabins, making it appear as if the cabins were part of the natural order of things. Corrals stood off to the side of the large equipment barn, and horses wandered through the snow, tossing their heads to and fro in delight.

She let her eyes take it all in, and she felt an ache deep inside for the eight years she'd been away from this. Home. Her heart knew it. Now, if she could just get her head to believe…*What? What did she want her head to believe? That she truly belonged here? Yes! Most definitely. That the mistakes of the past didn't matter? That too.*

She felt more tears spring to her eyes as her heart and her mind battled for supremacy.

That was how Mason found her moments later when he opened the back door to lift her from the vehicle. Crying. Again.

Chapter 13

Mason leaned his arms against the top of the vehicle door, and watched her with careful eyes. When Kaillar opened the door on the other side, Mason shook his head and gave him a look that only brothers would understand. *Leave. Now.*

Mason waited until Kaillar had gone inside and then he sighed, "Why are you crying? Is it your leg?" His tone of voice indicated that he already knew the answer.

Gracie looked at him, and felt bad for putting that cautious look in his eyes. "The lodge is beautiful."

He watched her for a moment and then laughed softly, "You're crying because you like the way the lodge looks?"

Gracie blushed and nodded her head, "Sorry. Maybe the pain meds don't agree with me? I seem to be on this emotional rollercoaster and I can't get off."

She was openly crying now, and Mason wrapped his arms around her, pulling her tear-stained face into his chest. "Shush. You can get off anytime you want."

"Can I? I don't think so."

"Gracie...let's go inside. I know Justin is anxious to see you, and he wants you to meet Jessica. Also, just to warn you – Melanie and her husband are here as well as Becca. Let's forget everything for the rest of the day and just try to enjoy each other, our family, and friends. Okay?"

Gracie pushed away from his chest, and used her fingertips to wipe the evidence of her tears away. "Okay." She took a breath and then looked up at him, "Any idea how I'm going to get out of here?"

Mason chuckled and then nodded, "Sit tight. I'm going to pull you out and carry you inside."

"You can't keep carrying me around," she argued, wrapping an arm around his shoulders anyway.

"Gracie, I will carry you for as long as you need me to."

She heard the double entendre in his words, but she chose to ignore it. "Well, I will accept that for the next little while, seeing as how I haven't any idea of how to walk around on crutches. And frankly," she looked around at the piles of snow everywhere, "is it even possible to walk on crutches in two feet of snow?"

Mason laughed, "Do me a favor and don't try? I would rather not make another trip to the hospital until your scheduled appointment."

"Deal. So, who is Jessica?"

Justin chose that moment to exit the house, no doubt wondering what was taking them so long to come inside. When he saw Mason carrying Gracie, he hurried down the steps to shut the car door and grab her stuff. "Hey! There she is. How you doing Gracie?"

"I'm going to be fine, Justin."

"Good to hear." He looked at Mason and inquired, "Everything else okay?"

Mason nodded, "Everything's fine. Since you're here, you can answer Gracie's question."

"What question?"

"Who is Jessica?" she asked, watching Justin's face go soft, and a slight blush stain his cheeks.

"Jessica is the woman I hope to marry one day in the near future."

"Wow! How long have you two been together?"

Justin's blush increased and then he cleared his throat, "There is nothing set in stone that says a couple must know each other for years before they know they're right."

Gracie nodded in agreement, as Mason climbed the stairs with her held securely in his arms. "You're right. There isn't. So, how long?"

"About a month." He smiled at her, and then openly laughed when he realized she wasn't going to lecture him.

Gracie raised a brow and then asked, "Are you sure she's the one?"

"Absolutely positive!"

Gracie smiled and relaxed in Mason's arms, "I'm happy for you. So, can we go inside now? I'm freezing."

Justin and Mason both started, and she chuckled as Justin hurried to open the door so that Mason could carry her inside. "Careful, don't bump her sore leg."

Mason froze, and then carefully walked them through the door frame, "Sorry. I didn't hurt you did I?"

Gracie shook her head, "No. I'm fine. In fact, you could put me down. I have to learn to get around on those crutches sometime. Six weeks is a long time. And before you offer, even you can't carry me around for six weeks."

Mason started to open his mouth, and then he realized how silly his protest would be. He couldn't carry her around for six weeks. He stood her up in the foyer, and then turned and accepted the crutches from Justin. They had been adjusted to the proper height back at the hospital, so all she had to do was slip them under her arms and start moving.

Gracie took a few hesitant steps, and then she looked up and saw everyone watching her, "Hey guys! Whoever said that doctors make the worst patients must have spoken from experience. Never again will I tell someone to stay off their feet for weeks, or hand them a set of crutches and blithely send them on their way. This is horrible!"

Everyone in the room started laughing and the tension dissipated that fast. Melanie and Becca both came over and hugged her, being careful not to disrupt her fragile balance. "I'm so glad you're going to be okay."

"I'm going to be fine. How are you?" She watched Becca blush and slip a glance towards Kaillar, but then she ducked her head and answered softly.

"I think I scared him by freaking out, but I'm fine now. A good night's sleep helped."

"Good. I have something I want to talk to you about before you guys head back to Denver."

Becca nodded, "We've been invited to stay for Thanksgiving dinner, so we aren't going back until Friday morning. Justin said you and Mason might be coming back then as well to get the rest of your things?"

"That's the plan." *I have some thinking to do before then, and I really need to talk to Doc. I want this to work. Maybe he'll have some great advice for me.*

"Good."

Justin walked over with a beautiful blonde's hand in his own, "Gracie this is Jessica Andrews. Jessica, this is Gracie Shelton."

Gracie smiled at the woman, and juggled her crutches until she could shake her hand. "Nice to meet you."

"You too. Justin has lunch ready. Are you hungry?"

Gracie looked up and then asked, "You cook?" She looked at Mason and shrugged her shoulders when he raised an eyebrow.

"Fine. I admit it. I thought you were joking about Justin cooking Thanksgiving dinner, and I really was expecting freeze-dried turkey and stuffing in one of those little foil bags."

Justin smiled and waggled his eyebrows at her, "I am a man of many talents. Come on. Get situated on the couch, and I'll have Mason bring you a plate."

Gracie followed his advice, and just like that, she felt the heavy burden of knowledge fall away to the back of her memory. She was going to live in the moment. At least for today.

Chapter 14

Wednesday morning…

Becca had just finished helping Gracie get dressed in a pair of borrowed sweat pants and a long sleeved t-shirt when they heard someone holler up the stairs that breakfast was ready. The two women made their way slowly into the large living area to see both Kaillar and Justin sitting at the table, along with Jessica, while Mason continued to make stacks of pancakes.

"You girls ready for breakfast?"

Gracie stopped and stared at him, "You cook?"

Mason smirked at her, "Thought you knew everything didn't you? And yes, I can cook. Have a seat."

Gracie looked at Justin, and shared a grin with him, "I kind of reminded him about his adventures in Home Ec while we were up in the shack."

Kaillar burst out laughing, "Oh man! I remember that. Uncle Jed was completely at a loss for words…"

Justin joined in and then whispered loudly, "We all started learning to cook right after that. Uncle Jed had several of the women from town come up and give us cooking lessons on the weekends and school vacations."

"I didn't know that," Gracie told him. She looked at Mason as he set a plate of pancakes in front of her, "How come I didn't know that?"

Mason tapped her on the nose, "There are lots of things you didn't get to know."

Gracie shook her head at him, "There can't be that many. From the time we were ten until I moved away, I practically lived up here."

Justin grinned, "Uncle Jed didn't seem to mind. He loved having you around. So, how is your knee this morning?"

Becca answered before she could, "She needs ice and elevation. She also needs some pain pills but after she eats."

"Are you my mother now?" Gracie asked on a laugh.

"No, but you've taken care of me enough times, I thought it was time to return the favor. I saw some board games on the bookshelf last night. Maybe we could play one after breakfast?"

"Monopoly?" Gracie asked with a twinkle in her eyes.

Becca groaned, "Sure. Why not? I like to lose."

"Do you guys have room for another player?" Jessica asked.

"Sure." Gracie looked around and then asked, "Where are Melanie and Michael?"

Justin grinned, "We set up the honeymoon suite for them. They have an entire cabin to themselves. Seemed only right to give them some quiet time together."

Gracie's heart melted and she reached across the table and covered Justin's hand with her own, "Thank you. I know that will mean the world to both of them. Before he came back to the States, Melanie did her best to stay positive, but every time there was another report of American soldiers dying, she would withdraw just a bit until the names were released. Then she would breathe easy for another few days, or weeks, and go through it all again."

Jessica shook her head, "I can't imagine how hard that must have been on her."

"But it all has a happy ending now. She's going to work for her dad in Florida, and Michael got his discharge, so they can be together now."

"More pancakes, anyone?" Mason asked, a spatula raised up above the skillet. When no one answered him, he turned the gas off and started cleaning up. Their Uncle Jed had been one smart cookie, and he'd quickly realized that boys who cleaned up after themselves in the kitchen learned the art of economy and multi-tasking with the cookware and utensils. The lodge had many modern appliances, but a dishwasher hadn't been added until Justin came home from the Middle East and the brothers decided to build their futures in Silver Springs.

Justin and Kaillar headed for the back door, grabbing jackets and gloves on their way out. "We're heading down to start the walks. Join us when you're done."

"Sure thing. I'll just make sure that the girls are set and be right out."

Becca, Jessica, and Gracie had already moved to the large couch, and were in the process of setting up the Monopoly board when he tossed the dish towel onto the hanging rack and joined them. "So, you girls need anything before I head outside?"

He'd watched Gracie shut down after she'd mentioned Melanie going to work for her dad. *Could this all have something to do with her father? She said she'd been fighting with him.*

"We're fine, thank you."

"Good. If you need anything, just let Jessica know. She's been up here enough that she knows where most things are located."

Gracie watched him from beneath her lashes as he slipped his jacket on, and then grabbed his gloves. He gave her one last searching glance before shaking his head and stepping outside.

"What was that all about?" Jessica asked once he was gone.

"What are you talking about?" Gracie asked.

"Come on. We might not know each other, but I do know some of Mason's tells. What's with all the looks? At times Mason looks completely happy, and then he watches you and looks like someone kicked his new puppy."

Gracie dropped her eyes, "It's complicated."

Jessica nodded her head and then suggested, "So uncomplicate it."

Becca took her hand, "Do you remember what you told me? After the…" She cleared her throat, glanced at Jessica, and then finished her sentence, "After I was attacked?"

Gracie shook her head, "Not really."

"Well, I do. I kept saying that it was all my fault. That I should have been more careful, and you got mad at me. You were almost yelling at me because I wouldn't listen to you. You said…you said that I didn't make the choice to be attacked. I made the choice to walk through the parking garage to get to my car. A perfectly normal activity that should have been safe.

"But the men who attacked me, they also made a decision that night. One that ended up hurting me and costing them their freedom. It didn't take right then, but over the next few days, I kept hearing you telling me that it wasn't my fault. That I didn't do anything to deserve getting attacked."

"Do you believe me now?" Gracie asked, her voice full of compassion at what Becca had gone through.

"I do. Now, I want to return the favor. Tell me what's going on between you and Mason. Please let me help you."

Gracie sighed, the board game forgotten. She looked up, and then shook her head, "Nothing's wrong." She'd enjoyed breakfast, the easy banter between her and everyone else. She wanted to continue basking in the warmth and love the Donnelly boys offered, and thoughts of the past would ruin that.

"Let's play," she said a bit too gaily. *One more day? Please God, just one more day before I have to start thinking about the future.*

Chapter 15

Mason grabbed a snow shovel, and started in on a section of the walkways that was still covered in snow. He could see Justin and Kaillar up ahead, and made it his personal goal to finish before them. Even though he'd gotten a late start.

That's how it had always been. The three boys challenging each other to be better, faster, smarter. Everything had been turned into a competition, and their Uncle Jed had been an expert at harnessing that competitive spirit and teaching them how to win and lose with grace.

Mason tossed his hands up as he finished two shovelfuls ahead of Justin, and five ahead of Kaillar. He and his brothers headed to the equipment barn, with Mason pulling out three sodas from the fridge kept there.

He popped the top, and hauled himself up to sit on a hay bale. "So, Becca seems more stable today."

Kaillar nodded, "Yeah, she slept well the first night, and seems to be handling being around me a little better."

"That's good news. Any idea of what happened to her yet?"

"Melanie kind of filled me in. She was attacked a few months ago in a parking garage. The attack stole her confidence, and Gracie diagnosed her as suffering from PTSD. She refuses to get some help, and according to Melanie, she refused to call her parents and tell them what had happened."

"That doesn't sound good."

"No. It isn't. But I'm not going to worry about it. I could see myself getting to know a girl like her, but she lives in Denver, and I already know I'm not up for a long distance relationship. Besides, she needs someone who's going to be around all the time."

Mason and Justin nodded, in agreement with his assessment. Changing the subject, Mason asked, "You up for a trip to Denver Friday morning?"

Justin nodded, "Yeah. Jessica will probably want to tag along as well."

"Good. I figured we'd take the small trailer and bring back whatever belongings she's bringing here."

"That's doable. You planning to spend the night?"

Mason shook his head, "I wasn't really planning on it."

"Well, do so. You in, Kai?"

"No. I'm scheduled to act as ski patrol all weekend. You guys go and have fun. I think Melanie and her hubby are heading out Friday morning as well. That probably means that Becca will be out of here as well."

Justin nodded and then turned to Mason, "So what happened up at the hospital?"

Mason looked up at the rafters and then shook his head, "Wish I knew. Something about mom."

"Whose mom?" Justin asked for clarification.

"Our mother. Gracie told the nurse that she is responsible for mom's death."

Justin said nothing and then he suggested, "Think she needs to talk to someone about the thoughts in her head?"

"You mean like a shrink?" Mason asked, already shaking his head, completely against the idea.

"No. Like a pastor. Or Doc. Both men could provide an unbiased ear to listen. As well as some valuable insight and good advice."

Mason thought for a moment, "That's not a bad idea. Doc was alive when mom was growing up and Jeremy wasn't. That would provide Gracie with two different viewpoints on whatever's bothering her.

"I told her she never had to tell me whatever it is. She seems to think it will change how I think about her, but I've assured her it wouldn't. I don't think she believes me."

Justin smiled, "Leave it to me. Jeremy and his family are already planning to join us for dinner tomorrow. Doc Matthews already had plans, but I could probably get him to drop by and visit his replacement later this afternoon."

Kaillar smiled, "Throw in dinner, and I can guarantee he'll be here."

Justin laughed; everyone in Silver Springs knew the best way to get around Doc Matthews was through his stomach. The man loved food, and Justin had often wondered how he stayed in such good shape, eating the way he did.

"I'm cooking steak tonight, baked potatoes with all the fixings, and some greens. I'll call Doc as soon as I get back into the house. I promised I'd take Jessica and Becca out in one of the snow machines this afternoon. Becca is a photographer, and is hoping to catch some wildlife shots for her portfolio."

Mason looked at Kaillar, who was listening to the conversation about Becca. *There's more than a passing interest there. Very interesting.*

The three men headed back into the lodge half an hour later, the sound of the girls giggling uproariously over something that eluded them immediately grabbing their attention. Stopping in the doorway, they asked, "Girls? What's so funny?"

Justin walked over and sat down behind Jessica, pulling her back against his knees, "So who is winning?"

That question caused more giggles to erupt. "Okay. Let me rephrase my question. Are you even playing?"

Again, more giggles. He stood up and then shook his head at them, "I'll let you three help each other out with the explanations then." He kissed Jessica on the top of her head, and then sauntered off, with Kaillar right behind him.

That left Mason alone with the three women, and he immediately grabbed one of their tea cups to see if they'd gotten into the cooking brandy kept in the kitchen. It was one of the few alcoholic beverages that could be found on the premises, and was only used very rarely.

Jessica sobered and trailed after Justin, "See you girls later." Becca took one look at Mason's face, and scampered after her as if she were being chased by a pack of hounds.

"Well! I guess that just leaves you to explain all of the laughter," Mason told her.

Gracie took one look at his face and then she stopped laughing, growing sober, and feeling that terrible weight from her conscience weighing her down.

"Whoa! Stop! Whatever is going through your mind, just stop it."

Gracie gave him a sad look, and then lowered her eyes to her lap. "I'm trying."

Mason moved so that he was sitting right next to her. He carefully wrapped an arm around her shoulders, "I know. Justin is inviting Doc up here for dinner. We all thought you might want a chance to talk to him, and getting around town right now is going to be more than difficult."

Gracie smiled at him and nodded, "Thank you. So, tell me about the other changes that have happened to Silver Springs. Jessica said she's the new elementary teacher?"

Mason released her shoulders, and spent the next hour trying to catch her up about the town and its inhabitants. Some minor things had changed while she'd been gone, but very few major things had. Silver Springs was still just a small Colorado mountain town.

After filling her in on the important facts, he stood up and then scooped her into his arms.

"Wait! Where are you taking me?"

"To the kitchen. I'm making lunch, and you are going to watch and be amazed," he predicted.

"Oh really? This I definitely have to see." She paused for effect, and then lowered her voice, "You're not making a cake are you?"

Mason tickled her ribs, and set her down at the large island. He handed her a cutting board, a knife, and a pile of vegetables. "Chop."

Gracie smiled and then asked, "What are we making?"

"Chicken noodle soup and cheese sandwiches."

"Yum." Gracie chopped vegetables, and watched Mason move confidently around the kitchen. She watched him add spices without measuring, and found herself smiling and relaxing in his presence.

When the soup was all put together and left to simmer on the stove, Mason covered it, and then turned to her with a smile on his face, "Want to go play in the snow?"

"Uhm…no! Not with this knee. I'm happy to watch from the window though, while you build me a snowman."

Mason grinned and scooped her back up into his arms. He deposited her in a chair facing the large picture windows, and helped her prop her knee up on the ottoman. He grabbed a bag of ice for her, and then kissed her nose, "One snowman coming up. Watch and be amazed!"

Gracie did watch, and she was amazed. Amazed that she'd managed to survive away from this place for so long. Silver Springs was home, and she just needed to find a way to deal with the past and move forward. *Like her mother had done.*

Chapter 16

Doc Matthews didn't need a second invite, and around 2 o'clock Wednesday afternoon, he arrived at the Three Brothers Lodge with a smile on his face and several questions rolling around in his brain.

"She's right in here," Justin informed the older man.

Gracie looked up from the book she'd been pretending to read to see a familiar face beaming at her from the doorway. "Doc! I'd get up to greet you, but as you can see, I've decided to find out what it's like to be on the other side of the exam table."

Doc came over to the couch and seated himself on a side chair, barely noticing when Justin slipped away from the room. "I'll tell you a little secret. When I was just out of my residency, I thought I had the world by the tail. Then I got too cocky and fell off a horse."

He laughed at himself, "I spent two weeks in the hospital with my leg in traction, and another three months hobbling around in a full leg cast. When I was finally able to start rehab, I had a much better understanding of what my patients were going through, and it changed the way I did medicine."

Gracie nodded her head, "I can already tell you I feel the same way. I will never prescribe a patient stay off their feet again without understanding how difficult a task that truly is."

Doc smiled at her and then asked a few questions about the surgery and her prognosis before inquiring, "So, how does it feel to be back in Silver Springs? You were fourteen when your parents uprooted you. A difficult time to be sure."

Gracie sighed, "To tell you the truth, all I've thought about since we left, was coming back. Part of me loves being back here. The town. The mountains."

"The men?" Doc questioned. "I seem to remember you and young Mason were inseparable. And he's the one who rescued you on the mountain, correct?" When she nodded, he looked at her and then asked, "Sparks still there?"

She closed her eyes briefly and nodded, "In some ways it's like I never left. But…"

Doc sat back and then sighed, "You can't get past what you know that he doesn't." It was a statement and not a question.

Gracie looked up at him in shock and questioned, "How…I mean,.."

Doc gave her a sad look, "Give an old man a moment to clear his conscience, will you?"

"Okay."

"Let me tell you another story. About a young woman who hated the simple living of Silver Springs. She had stars in her eyes, and a desire to be sought after for all the wrong reasons. She bolted from here just as soon as she could, seeking fame and fortune in the big city.

"But as is wont to happen in such cases, she was naïve and ripe for the picking by every user she met. Fame was elusive, and fortune just a myth. She ended up buying the snake oil that was sold as a cure all for her ills. But all it brought was further destruction and addictions that ruled her life.

"Then came the decisive moment when she had to think of someone other than herself. And she made the right choice. She came back to Silver Springs, but soon the allure of the bright lights and big city drew her back.

"This destructive cycle continued. No matter how many times she was rescued, she was never able to abandon her yearning to be somewhere else."

He paused and Gracie shook her head, "That is such a sad story. Was she someone close to you?"

Doc shook his head, "Not in the way you're thinking. When I first came to Silver Springs thirty-seven years ago, this young lady was eight. I watched her grow up, as I did so many young people in and around this town. When she came back home, I helped her parents try to deal with her addictions, but those were only physical things. Her mind was the real problem, and psychiatry is not my specialty."

"What happened to her?" Gracie asked, still not having put the pieces together.

"She died. Alone. Probably afraid. Her choices came back to seek their revenge, and she paid with her life."

"Her parents must have been so sad."

"Fortunately, God was gracious and neither of them lived to see their daughter's ultimate fall. See, she'd been raised in a good Christian household. Was a member of the youth group, and had parents who loved and cared for her. She even had a brother who would do anything to help her out. None of that made a difference."

"I don't get how someone who was raised one way can abandon everything and go so far in the opposite direction."

"Have you talked with Jessica?" he inquired.

"Just a few minutes here and there."

"Her parents were missionaries to South Africa. They were murdered, and she spent years running from God, blaming Him for taking her parents away from her. Blaming Him for leaving her all alone."

"She doesn't seem bitter."

"Not today. That's because she finally decided that the past belongs precisely there. In the past. But, I digress. There's more to my story.

"The young woman was like a bad apple. Even though she came home humbled and trying to do the right thing, she never let go of her desire for a different lifestyle. Over the years, there were people whose lives were sullied by her. By her actions.

"See, this young woman's conscience had been seared, and she no longer held to the traditional concepts of right and wrong. Black and white. And in any group of people, there are always those whose will to withstand temptation is weak and untried. It was those people that she appealed to and took down to her level."

Gracie was trying to understand, "She brought drugs to Silver Springs?" She wasn't aware there was a drug problem in the small town. It wouldn't surprise her overly much, but it would still be worrisome to her.

"No. It wasn't the drugs she brought; it was her addiction to personal pleasure. Her selfishness when it came to respecting marriage vows."

Gracie suddenly felt uncomfortable. Her father had been such a man; weak. All too willing to abandon his marriage vows for a few brief moments of pleasure. "Did these men ever get found out?"

Doc sighed, "Some. Others went to great lengths to hide their transgressions. Even going so far as to uproot their family overnight with the mistaken notion that they could leave their actions and guilt behind just as easily."

Gracie looked at the older man with wide open eyes, "You knew."

Doc nodded his head, "I suspected. When your dad took you and your mom away so suddenly, I was sure."

"My dad...it was years after we left before he finally confessed to my mom and me. He told us how he'd been consumed by guilt and called things off with her. She'd been upset and taken off for Las Vegas. Where she'd died several days later."

"Her choice. Remember that."

"My father's choice. A choice that caused Maria to rush away..."

"She would have left anyway. It wasn't in her nature to stay. Gracie, look at me." He waited until she did so, "If you are carrying any guilt around for your father's actions, you need to let it go. You can't re-write history. You don't deserve to live under that kind of shadow."

"Deserve? Did Mason or his brothers deserve to grow up motherless?"

"Even if she'd lived, those boys would have stayed with their uncle. He loved them, Maria loved herself."

Mason stood in the doorway and spoke up just then, "Doc's right, you know. My mother was the most selfish woman I've ever heard of." Mason came and sat down next to her, "Is that the secret you've been afraid to share? That your father cheated on your mother with mine? Trust me; we've heard it all before. Our mother had no morals, and even less of a conscience."

"But, my father said that she was upset when he called the dalliance off, and that's what sent her running back to Las Vegas. Where she died."

"No, sugar. Her addiction and lifestyle choices drew her back to Las Vegas. Your father was just a pawn, used by her for her own means."

Gracie stared at him, barely registering when Doc left the room, leaving her alone with Mason and her chaotic thoughts. "I was sure you'd hate me when you found out what my father had done."

"I'm hurt you didn't trust me more, but I also understand that you've lived with this knowledge for a while, and didn't truly know how messed up our mother was." Mason looked at her and then held open his arms, "Gracie, I have never allowed my mother's sins to affect my life. Can you do the same with your father's sins?"

Gracie was once again crying, sobbing actually at the sense of relief she felt. For the first time since hearing of her father's actions, she didn't feel guilty. Hearing Mason, as he continued to murmur to her, saying that he cared about her, and not about the actions of her father, was like a balm being applied to a fresh wound.

"I'm sorry," she cried against his chest. "I'm sorry I didn't have the guts to just tell you what I knew and trust you to deal with the information correctly."

"Don't be. We have eight years to make up for. We are going to make up for them, aren't we?"

"I'd like that."

Mason hugged her close, and then pushed her back to tip her eyes up to meet his own. He touched her lips with a fingertip and then asked, "I gave you your first kiss. Can I give you another one now?"

Gracie didn't wait for him to act, she lifted her mouth towards his, meeting him as he lowered his lips to take hers in a sweet kiss full of promise and love.

The door in her heart swung wide open, and she could honestly say she was now at home. Silver Springs was going to become her new place of residence, but wherever Mason was would always be home.

Chapter 17

Thanksgiving Day…

"All right everyone. Dinner's ready."

Mason scooped Gracie up and placed her in the chair that had been set at the end of the long dining table. By turning just a tad sideways, she'd be able to keep her leg elevated and still join everyone else at the table. Mason took the chair right next to her, making sure that he could easily help her if she required it.

Gracie grinned at him and whispered, "You do realize it's my knee that's hurt and not my hands. Or my arms. Or my head?"

Mason blushed, "I just have this need to take care of you. Enjoy it."

Gracie kissed him on the cheek, "I am."

Justin stood up and looked around the table. Jessica was seated to his right. Kaillar was seated to his left with Becca, Melanie and Michael rounding out that side of the table. Sarah sat next to Jessica, and Scott Taylor and his wife Chloe finished that side of the table. Their newborn baby sat on a chair between them, sleeping peacefully in a carrier.

"Shall we say grace?" Everyone bowed their head and Justin raised his voice up, "Father, on this day of Thanksgiving, we remember the many blessings You have brought our way this past year. The relationships You've restored, the new ones You've brought into our lives."

"We especially offer up thanks for bringing Gracie back home to us. Now as we eat together, we ask that Your hand would stay upon us and guide us in the coming year to do Your will and help our fellow man."

"Amen."

Everyone looked up and the feast began. Gracie watched as bowls of food were passed around, and laughter seemed to be the mode of the day. She'd missed this. After leaving Silver Springs, her home had become very tense and strained. Her mother had tried to make it like it was before, but that had been impossible.

When Gracie had been offered a full-ride scholarship with room and board, she'd jumped at the chance to get away from the oppressive atmosphere of her home. But she'd been years younger than her classmates and more of an oddity and someone to be pitied than someone to hang out with. Loneliness had become the norm.

"You okay?" Mason murmured to her, scooping potatoes onto her still empty plate.

"Just thinking how nice it is to be here with you all. I missed this."

Mason smiled at her, "You're home now and you never have to leave again."

"I don't?" she teased him.

Mason grew very serious, and then he looked down at his plate for a moment. When he looked back up, Gracie saw something in his eyes she'd never seen before. Emotion and a yearning that tugged at her heart.

"Gracie, I know this probably isn't the right time or place, but waiting around for that doesn't seem to always out so well for us. So...I don't want you to ever leave. I guess what I'm saying is, I want us to be forever."

Gracie watched him with tear-filled eyes. She reached up to wipe them away and laughed, "Why am I always crying around you?"

"I don't know, but I promise to always be there to wipe them away. What do you say? Want to stay here forever with me? Like this? Gracie, will you marry me and make it official?"

Gracie nodded her head, happier than she'd ever been in her life. Mason tipped her chin up and kissed her, right there at the dinner table.

When the hoots and hollers of the others in the room reached their ears, Gracie turned bright red and bit her bottom lip. Mason absorbed their teasing as his due, "We're getting married!"

Justin and Kaillar both got up and hugged Gracie, "Welcome to the family sweetie!"

"Welcome home, Gracie girl."

"Thanks, guys. Let's eat."

Everyone got back to the act of eating dinner, and Gracie kept a careful eye on Becca. She'd sat down before Kaillar, and Gracie had seen the momentary look of panic on her friend's face when Kaillar had accidentally brushed her shoulder as he slipped into his chair.

She seemed to be handling things okay, but it was becoming very apparent to Gracie that Becca needed some professional help. And not on her timeframe. She needed help in the here and now.

As dinner wound down, Scott and Chloe disappeared to one of the guests rooms so that mommy and baby could both take a nap. Melanie and Michael returned to their small cabin with a plate of leftovers and orders not to return until 10 o'clock the next morning when everyone would be heading either to the ski slopes, back to town, or into Denver.

Sarah convinced Becca to come spend the night with her so that they could eat popcorn and watch sappy movies, and Gracie was happy to see a smile on her friend's face. Kaillar headed to the barn to get his skis ready for his work on the slopes the next morning, leaving Jessica, Justin, Mason, and Gracie in the house to fend for themselves.

Justin and Mason migrated towards the den and whatever football game happened to be still playing, and Jessica kept Gracie company. When she produce a tablet and brought up several stores in the Denver area that catered to off-the-rack wedding dresses, Gracie looked at her with a question in her eyes.

Jessica nodded her head, a happy smile on her face, "We were going to let it be a surprise once we got to Denver, but maybe we should both look at dresses while we're there?"

Gracie started giggling, and soon Jessica had joined her. The sounds of their laughter brought their men back in and once again, they couldn't seem to explain what was so funny.

Justin finally picked Jessica up and carried her out of the room, hoping that distance would help the two women get control of themselves. His actions caused another round of giggles.

Mason sat down next to Gracie, watching as she cried through her laughter and held her ribs because they hurt. "Is it something in the water, because I know you girls didn't consume any alcohol at dinner?"

Gracie shook her head, "I'm just happy. I'm not sure if that's what does it for Jessica, but I'm happy. Deliriously happy."

Mason smiled at her, "I can see that." He noticed the tablet on the ground, and picked it up, but the picture on the screen caused him to pause and look at her curiously.

"Jessica's idea. It seems that she and your brother have agreed to get married, but were waiting to keep it a secret. That's why he wanted to spend the night. So that they can fit the gown she chooses and she can bring it back with her."

Mason looked thoughtful, "Is that something you'd be interested in doing?"

Gracie watched him, "We haven't really talked about when and…"

"Today. Tomorrow. As soon as we can."

"I might need a bit more time than that. How about next week?"

"That sounds perfect."

"Then, yes. I'd like to look at dresses while we're in Denver tomorrow."

"Consider it done. You and Jessica can go dress shopping, and Justin and I will take care of packing up the rest of your things. Pick something pretty. Like you."

Gracie blushed, and then she couldn't think because he was kissing her. Life was perfect.

Epilogue

Adelaide's Wedding Shop, Friday afternoon…

"I really like this one with the full skirt," Jessica said, fingering the satin material of the ivory wedding dress. It had a sweetheart neckline, and tiny seed pearls attached in a delicate scroll pattern across the bodice and over the capped sleeves.

"That's gorgeous. You should definitely try that one on." Gracie was still trying to decide if she wanted to go traditional, or if she dared to find the dress she'd only dreamed about.

"Gracie?" Becca stood by her elbow, having decided that she would rather go dress shopping than sit at home by herself all day. Gracie was proud of her, and hoped to find time today to discuss her moving to Silver Springs and taking over for Sarah.

"Hey!"

"What kind of dress are you looking for?"

Gracie sighed, "I don't know."

Becca smiled at her, "I doubt that. Tell me about the dress you wear in your dreams."

Gracie grinned, "But that is only a dream dress. And they don't really exist."

"Tell me anyway, okay?"

"Velvet. In my dreams, my wedding dress is white velvet. It had a scoop neckline and lone sleeves with those little strings that hook over your middle finger to keep them in place. And a long skirt that swirls around my ankles when I walk, but drapes along the ground behind me."

"It sound gorgeous. Tiffany, do you have anything like that?" Becca asked the store attendant Gracie hadn't known was standing behind her listening in.

Tiffany smiled, "I have the perfect dress for you. Head on back to the dressing room, and I'll bring it to you."

Gracie looked at her, hope shining in her eyes, "You really have a dress like what I described?"

"Go on back and you'll see. It must have been made just for you."

Twenty minutes later, Gracie emerged from the dressing room, and everyone stopped and gasped at the picture she presented. She was stunning in the dress, and a more perfect fit didn't exist.

"Oh, Gracie! Look at yourself!" Jessica and Becca urged her.

Gracie took a breath and turned to face the three-way mirror. She gasped, and felt tears spring to her eyes. "It's perfect! Just like in my dreams."

Becca wrapped an arm around her waist, "Who was your perfect groom in your dreams?"

"Mason," Gracie whispered.

"A match made in heaven. She'll take it."

"Perfect." The store attendant was beaming as she walked away to start the paperwork.

"Now we have to find Jessica the perfect dress," Becca said.

"Well, I don't think I'm ever going to find anything as perfect as that one, but I have several to try on."

"Then get to it," Becca told her with a laugh.

Gracie changed back into her street clothes, and handed the gown over to be pressed one last time and then hung in a garment bag. Everything seemed to be going so well, and Jessica finally settled on a dress of her own that made her look like Cinderella ready for the ball.

They headed back to Jessica's apartment, and were pleased to see the boys loading the last of the boxes into the trailer.

"All done?" Gracie asked in wonder, glancing at her watch. They'd only been at it for three hours, but what they'd accomplished would have taken her three days. "Thank you."

"How about we go get some pizza?" Kaillar suggested, making sure that Becca knew she was invited as well.

"That sounds good. I know the perfect place just a few blocks down."

"Great."

Everyone started piling into the vehicles, but Becca's phone rang, and she hung back to answer it. Gracie watched her walk away before putting the phone to her ear. Becca's back stiffened, and then Gracie watched her phone drop to the ground.

"Becca!" Gracie sought Mason out, "Help her! What's wrong? Becca! Mason, take me to her."

Kaillar was closest and reached her first, catching her just as she fainted and would have hit the ground. "She's fainted."

Gracie waited impatiently while Kaillar and Justin checked her over. Kaillar picked her up, and settled her in the back of the vehicle next to Gracie. "What's wrong with her?"

"I don't know. Becca? Sweetie, open your eyes." Gracie looked up with worried eyes, "Where's her phone?"

"She dropped it." Kaillar retrieved it and then handed it over to Gracie. The screen was shattered, but Gracie ignored that and pulled up her most recent calls.

"Who just called her?" Justin asked, Jessica hanging on his arm.

Mason looked over Gracie's shoulder, "It say 'Mom'."

Gracie shook her head, "She doesn't talk to her parents. Not ever."

Becca moaned and began to come around. Gracie held onto her arm, and spoke softly to her, "Becca, you fainted. You're in the car with me. Who was on the phone?"

Becca stared straight ahead, "My mom."

"Your mom in Hawaii?" Gracie asked.

Becca nodded, "My dad's dead. The funeral is Sunday, and she wants me there."

Gracie's heart broke for her friend and she wrapped her in a hug, "Oh Becca. I'm so sorry. Honey, what can we do?"

Becca wasn't crying and that worried Kaillar more than the fact that she'd fainted. "She wants me to come for the funeral. I…"

"If money is a problem, I can lend you as much as you need.."

"No. I can…I just…," she looked up at Gracie with tears and fear in her eyes. "I can't go back there like this. Weak. I just can't. Not by myself. I…"

Gracie felt so helpless. With her knee, there was no way she could handle a journey to Hawaii. No way to get around on a plane, or…

She looked up and met Kaillar's eyes and saw the question there. She looked at Becca, who was unconsciously holding onto his hand. She nodded once, and Kaillar took over.

"Becca, darling. Do you want someone to go with you?"

Becca's mind was almost numb, but she nodded anyway. She raised teary eyes to him, and he felt a piece of his heart break away. "I'll take you home. Will you let me do that? Will you let me take you home to say goodbye to your dad?"

Becca shivered once, but she didn't look away from him. "Yes."

"Good. Justin, we need a ride to the airport."

"Done. We'll stop by her apartment and pack whatever she needs on the way. Jessica, would you mind finding the first flights out of here?"

"Not at all." She reached across and squeezed Becca's shoulder, "It's going to be all right. We're all here for you. It's what family does. They help each other in the good times and in the bad."

Thank You

Dear Reader,

Thank you for choosing to read my books out of the thousands that merit reading. I recognize that reading takes time and quietness, so I am grateful that you have designed your lives to allow for this enriching endeavor, whatever the book's title and subject.

Now more than ever before, Amazon reviews and Social Media play vital role in helping individuals make their reading choices. If any of my books have moved you, inspired you, or educated you, please share your reactions with others by posting an Amazon review as well as via email, Facebook, Twitter, Goodreads, -- or even old-fashioned face-to-face conversation! And when you receive my announcement of my new book, please pass it along. Thank you.

For updates about New Releases, as well as exclusive promotions, visit my website and sign up for the VIP mailing list. Click here to get started: www.morrisfenrisbooks.com

I invite you to connect with me through Social media:

1. Facebook   :
   https://www.facebook.com/AuthorMorrisFenris/
2. Twitter: https://twitter.com/morris_fenris
3. Pinterest: https://www.pinterest.com/AuthorMorris/
4. Instagram:
   https://www.instagram.com/authormorrisfenris/

For my portfolio of books on Amazon, please visit my Author Page:

Amazon USA:
amazon.com/author/morrisfenris

Amazon UK:
https://www.amazon.co.uk/MorrisFenris/e/B00FXLWKRC

You can also contact me by email:
authormorrisfenris@gmail.com

With profound gratitude, and with hope for your continued reading pleasure,

Morris Fenris
Author & Publisher

26339484R00069

Printed in Great Britain
by Amazon